GREAT B
EXPLO

SECRETS OF AYDAGAR

Calee Bryce

ISBN:
Paperback: 978-1-80227-012-9
eBook: 978-1-80227-013-6

Cover illustration from original artwork by Sofia Evlo
The right of Calee Bryce to be identified as the author and illustrator
of this work has been asserted.

Find out more about Calee Bryce at
www.caleebryce.com

First published in May 2020

For my four boys
– Orestes, Stefanos, Maximillian, Cristopher –
as well as
every other child starting out on the amazing
adventure called life.

CONTENTS

WIGMORE ABBEY

POWER COAST

MONSTER CAVES

AVATON TOWERS

Aydagar

Monster Caves

Avaton Towers

Arnce

Tree House

Andria

Camp

Power Coast

N
W E
S

WIGMORE ABBEY

1

HOW IT ALL BEGAN

Isabelle sat quietly at the back of the small vehicle, sandwiched in between two suitcases, clutching a small floppy bag on her lap. Her mother eased herself behind the wheel and slammed the door shut. After adjusting her lipstick in the rear-view mirror, she glanced back at her daughter.

'Let's be on our way then. The sooner we get you there, the more time you'll have to settle in.'

'Where's pop?' said Isabelle. 'Isn't he going to see me off?'

'Who knows where your father is,' her mother said, bluntly.

Growing up, Isabelle's father would spend as much time as he could with her. He was always taking her places, reading her bedtime stories and making sure he had breakfast with her every day.

But recently, he was always gone; leaving the house at the crack of dawn and returning well after she was asleep.

Whenever Isabelle asked what was happening, her mother would either start crying or change the subject.

And if that wasn't bad enough, Isabelle was now being

trundled off to a snobby boarding school, far away from home, in the middle of nowhere.

'It'll be like going to prison,' said Isabelle.

'Don't be silly. Of course, it won't. You'll learn lots of things that I never had a chance to learn. And think of all the lovely people you'll meet,' her mother said cheerily.

'But I don't want to meet new people. I just want my friends.'

'Oh Isabelle, you don't know what you want.'

'You never listen to me,' said Isabelle, under her breath.

She flung herself back into the car seat with a groan, as her mother started the engine, and sped off down the gravel driveway.

Looking out of the car window, the trees along the side of the road seemed to whiz by like blurs. Not paying much attention to what she saw, Isabelle's mind started to replay the events that had transpired over the last two months.

'Your father and I are getting a divorce. Not right away, but soon.'

'What?' said Isabelle, completely lost for words.

She put her hands to her face and burst into tears.

'Sometimes in life, Isabelle dearest, we have to decide what we can live with and what we can't,' said her mother, trying to explain the situation.

The words coming into Isabelle's ears became fuzzy and indistinct and she felt herself being pushed into a big, black hole.

Her mother sat down next to her and touched her arm, but Isabelle stiffened and pulled away.

'Isabelle, it is what it is,' her mother said in a harsh, Scottish lilt. 'Your father is moving out of the house and I have to find work.'

'Where, em, am I going to stay?' Isabelle asked, between sobs.

'Well, you're a very lucky girl because you're going to Wigmore Abbey.'

'What's that?' asked Isabelle.

'It's a super boarding school, just by the sea.'

A look of panic crossed Isabelle's face.

'But why? Why can't I go to school here, with my friends?'

'Because you'll get a much better education at Wigmore,' said her mother.

'But you don't understand …' said Isabelle.

'I don't need to understand. The decision has been made.'

There wasn't an ounce of uncertainty in her mother's voice and all of Isabelle's protests fell on deaf ears. She wanted so much to say, 'I won't go,' but just couldn't come out with it. But then again, Isabelle never had the confidence to really stand up to her mother and say 'No, I won't do this,' or 'I don't care about that.'

Most times she did as she was asked, becoming an invisible Isabelle. She simply got used to allowing people, especially her mother, to look past her, never seeing who she truly was or what she really wanted.

Isabelle had also learnt from her parents that it was easier not to talk about problems or feelings.

In fact, they never really talked about anything and if there was something her parents didn't agree on, they would simply back off for fear of igniting an argument. Ignoring each other until enough time had passed that they could forget about the problem seemed quite normal.

Everything was so different now from what Isabelle had planned during her summer holidays. She was ready to move on to high school with the friends that she had had such difficulty making. Now, when she had finally achieved a sense of belonging, her life was being taken from her as she found herself thrown into a whirlwind turn of events.

It was nearly three hours of travelling through hilly countryside before Isabelle and her mother arrived at the high stone walls surrounding the grounds of Wigmore Abbey. Turning into a huge wrought iron gateway, they drove through the vast school grounds, down a long avenue flanked on either side by lime trees. Isabelle's eyes remained fixed to the perimeter wall, trying to figure out how easy it would be to climb over.

They passed several smaller houses until they reached the courtyard of the main school. The exterior of the three-storey building was imposing, with a tower looming over the main entrance and turrets on each corner.

'This looks worse than a prison. It's more like a torture chamber,' Isabelle said.

'Nonsense and don't be so ungrateful,' her mother snapped. 'Now, out you get. And remember, stand up straight, no more slouching.'

As Isabelle got out of the car, she looked up at a tall double-sash window, where some pale faces were looking down at her.

'Are they ghosts?' she said.

'Oh Isabelle, you have such a silly imagination,' her mother said dismissively.

A few introductions were followed by a flying kiss and a quick wave goodbye, and in no time at all, the family car sped away as fast as the wind would allow. Isabelle soon found herself in a bare bedroom with seven other girls, confined to a cold, medieval manor house in the middle of nowhere.

After just a few months as a boarder, Isabelle's confidence

started to crack as she struggled to fit in. She was not the quickest academically and often got left behind in class.

'But I tried Miss, I really did,' Isabelle said, after getting a D for her English test.

'Obviously not hard enough,' said Ms Britain, her nostrils quivering. 'Have you ever been tested for learning disabilities?'

'N - no Miss,' answered Isabelle, feeling afraid and embarrassed.

Ms Britan's glare bored into Isabelle's head, reminding her of a story her father had told her of Medusa; a winged female monster from Greek mythology, who used to turn anyone gazing into her eyes into stone. Isabelle immediately looked down and closed her eyes tight, just in case.

The only way Isabelle could express her frustration in this new world of discipline, punishment and grim food was to build an invisible fence around herself, pretending not to see or care.

But there was a light at the end of Isabelle's very dark tunnel; her two new friends, Akira and Holly.

'There's no way I can stand six more years of this,' Isabelle told them.

'But there are so many great things about this school,' said Akira, in her perfectly British accent.

She eyed Isabelle with her dark brown, almond-shaped, Asian eyes.

'Like what?' said Isabelle. 'The rooms are freezing, the food is crap and most of the teachers are old, strict, weird and scary.'

'Not all of them,' said Akira.

'Just about most of them,' said Isabelle. 'Mr Wheeler's a perv, Miss Lancaster is always criticising and telling us off, and what about Miss Unwin? She's got hairs sprouting out of her nostrils and her armpit sweat oozes through her shirts and leaves those icky yellow stains.'

'I personally would just call her a little eccentric,' said Akira.

'The only one that's kind and nice to me is Miss Barnden, the drama teacher,' said Isabelle.

'Izzy's got a point. Mr Michael's also a bit whacky, always threatening us with his horsewhip,' said Holly.

'Discipline is important,' said Akira.

'Seriously?' gasped Isabelle.

'We'll be fine, if we all stick together,' said Holly.

Always bubbly and bright, Holly was the life and sole of the trio. Given the chance, the three of them could talk and talk about everything under the sun, moon and stars for hours on end.

Most days, Isabelle would also try and keep happy by wrapping herself in a fleecy blanket of stories about mythological beings and legendary creatures. But even those stories couldn't help her shake off the sadness that she felt on this particular day.

It was the eve of her twelfth birthday, and there was no one from the outside world to remember the fact; not even her parents. Just a big, fat silence that filled the gloomy corridors and dormitories of Wigmore Abbey.

'Didn't I get any letters, or cards?' Isabelle said, her eyes flicking automatically to her empty pigeonhole.

'Nope, nothing, zilch,' replied the tall, scary looking prefect in charge of the daily post.

'Maybe they got mixed up with …' Isabelle started.

'I never make mistakes when it comes to my duties,' the sixth former replied, curtly.

It was Isabelle's worst ever birthday.

Checking one final time to make sure that everyone in her

dormitory was sound asleep, Isabelle quietly got out of bed. Pulling the duvet over her shoulders, she crept barefoot across the room towards a tall bay window. Each step she took was precise, so as not to make any of the old floorboards creak.

Slipping behind the thick curtains, Isabelle perched herself on the wide windowsill, drawing her skinny legs up to her chest and wrapping her arms around them. She snuggled under her duvet and leaned forward to rest her chin on her knees.

This was Isabelle's usual thinking position, in her most favourite thinking spot. She had spent many nights over the last three months tucked away here, dreaming up schemes of escape from this awful place.

She pressed her nail-bitten finger into the condensation on the window and traced the words Happy B-day Izzy. Biting down hard on her bottom lip, Isabelle swallowed a sob that had lodged in her throat. With her open palm she began to forcefully wipe the words off the glass, smearing the condensation in a slow and circular motion.

Sighing loudly, her warm breath turned to small clouds as it left her mouth. Isabelle's hazel eyes, the only characteristic she had inherited from her father, filled with salty tears and dribbled down her slightly acne-pitted cheeks.

'What's that?' she thought, squinting through her tears.

Whilst wiping her eyes Isabelle noticed, in the distance, a white light flashing. It seemed to be moving closer and closer, towards the shoreline.

Pushing some stray strands of hair behind her ear, she looked out again, but the light had gone. All she could now see was the glimmer of water shining under the moon and the mist crawling across the sea.

'Probably a fishing trawler,' she mumbled, under her breath.

Isabelle rested her head against the window-frame and drew in a stuttering breath. Her stinging eyes began to slowly close as she found herself wishing she could travel into the future. She wished she was more like her two new friends; clever and bold, like Akira, popular and pretty, like Holly. She wished she could get rid of the sad feelings that were brewing inside her and just feel happy again.

'I wish I could go somewhere far, far away,' were her last jumbled thoughts before drifting off to sleep.

Then, all of a sudden, in that dreamlike state, just before entering deep sleep, Isabelle felt a pressure against her toes. At first, she felt too weighed down by drowsiness to react, but then she jerked awake and poked her head out from under her duvet.

Sitting exactly opposite her was a very pale, ghostlike figure that looked remarkably like a cartoon-version of herself. It was like looking into a mirror. Reflected back at her was a semi-transparent girl of similar build, with wavy brown hair like hers, and almost the same colour eyes.

Running her finger over a dent in her right cheek, Isabelle noticed that they even had the same, single dimple. As she searched for words that just wouldn't come, the figure looked at Isabelle, her eyes bright with excitement.

'I'm Whisper!'

Giggles bubbled up from her throat, and she let off a tinkling sound, like glass chimes.

Tinkle, tinkle, ting-a-ling.

'*Haaa!*' Isabelle gasped, and then stayed silent for a few seconds.

Her sense of curiosity was, however, far stronger than her surprise, so Isabelle couldn't help but want to know what or who this Whisper was.

'Wh - who?' she asked, stammering, but finally finding her voice.

'I am you and you are me, connected to each other since the day we were born,' answered Whisper.

Isabelle hesitated, trying to make sense of what Whisper had just said.

'But I don't remember you,' said Isabelle.

It all seemed so unreal, so out of this world. Yet Isabelle felt a strange, inexplicable sense of familiarity and comfort that all was well and as it should be. She pulled back the curtain slightly, peeking to see if anyone had woken up. Everyone was fast asleep.

'I am an invisible energy in you,' Whisper continued.

Isabelle sat with a dazed look on her face. She yanked a tuft of her hair to make sure she was awake. This made Whisper laugh, setting off her chimes once again.

Tinkle – tinkle – ting-a-ling.

'You mean, you're like my spirit?' Isabelle said, scrunching up her nose.

A broad grin spread across Whisper's face once again as she answered.

'In a way, yes. You can also call me your intuition.'

'My intuition?'

Isabelle quietly repeated the word a few times, whilst searching her memory.

'Oh, yes.'

She had heard the word, knew it was something inside her, but didn't quite know what it meant. Whisper explained that she was the wise spirit inside of Isabelle that had always been by her side since birth, whispering in her thoughts and guiding her through her everyday life.

'I am the real you that has always been,' said Whisper.

'Aren't I the real me that I've always been?' said Isabelle, with a quick shake of her head.

'Of course, you are. But something is different now,' said Whisper.

'What d'you mean?' said Isabelle.

'You're growing up,' answered Whisper.

From the time Isabelle was around six years old, she would instinctively listen to Whisper's secret voice inside her head, showing her the right way. But the older she became, the self-doubt that Isabelle started experiencing in her life began to weaken the bond between the two of them.

Slowly but surely Isabelle, as with so many others of her age, had almost stopped listening to Whisper altogether. As a result, she had begun to believe in herself less and less; gradually becoming more and more unhappy.

'Who you think you are, Izzy, has hidden what you really are from view,' said Whisper.

'She knows my nickname!' thought Isabelle.

'Of course, I do!' Whisper responded.

The sound of *tinkle, tinkle, ting-a-ling* rang out as her reflection laughed again.

Whisper could always read Isabelle's mind and knew her better than anyone else; better than her beating heart and her spinning mind. She also knew all too well that once they both became deeply re-connected, Isabelle would start trusting, believing in, and revealing her true self again.

'You can also think of me as your inner guide,' Whisper said, as if she was disclosing a secret.

Isabelle's eyes grew huge at the thought of having something so awesome inside of her.

'Stay close to me, Izzy. Listen carefully and you will find all the ways to feel good once again,' said Whisper.

'Can you really make that happen?'

'Together we can make it happen,' answered Whisper.

It was, after all, Isabelle's wish to feel happy and carefree once again. A smile that came from an excitement and hope deep inside lit up Isabelle's face.

'But, how?' she asked.

Whisper smiled and tipped her head, giving the most unexpected answer.

'By travelling to a faraway land beyond the earthly realm, to Aydagar.'

2

THE DECISION

'Ay - da - gar!' Isabelle said, with a sigh.

'Yes, an island that lies under the Great Atlantic Sea, and welcomes only those who are brave of heart and are willing to have an open mind.'

Isabelle nibbled her bottom lip while she tried to get her jumbled thoughts in order. It was difficult to know what she felt exactly. Whisper seemed like an angel in Isabelle's eyes; wise, kind and loving.

She felt reassured and yet a bit fearful, full of questions. How would she get to this place? Would she be alone? What if someone found out that she was gone? And more importantly, did she have a brave heart, or even an open mind?

'I still don't get it. Why me?' asked Isabelle.

'Why not you? Izzy, this is your chance to learn about just how extraordinary you are. You are so very much more than you think you are,' she continued.

Isabelle sat still for a moment more, thinking everything over, until her head slowly started to clear.

'Is it just me, I mean, that's got special powers?'

'Everybody has them, Izzy. But only a few people have had the chance to discover them and become the amazing person they were born to be,' said Whisper.

'How come?'

'Some people have simply never been told,' said Whisper. 'And others may have been told about the powers within themselves, but weren't ready to listen, ready to understand, or even ready to believe.'

Now Isabelle had even more questions, but when she opened her mouth, she found she couldn't speak.

'And most people have never been willing to break a few rules,' said Whisper.

She held her hand over her mouth and chuckled as she thought about Isabelle sneaking out of school.

'But what happens if I get caught?' she said. 'I'll get into so much trouble.'

'Nobody will even realise you're gone,' said Whisper, reassuringly. 'From the moment we leave here and until our return, time as you know it will stand still.'

Isabelle played with her hair absentmindedly, hardly daring to believe that all this stuff about a fantastical land and time standing still could be true.

'She doesn't realise I'm not good enough,' she thought silently.

Whisper looked at Isabelle with her penetrating green-brown eyes and with a silent voice responded telepathically.

'You most certainly are.'

'I heard that in my head,' said Isabelle, surprised.

'Of course, you did. Remember, I'm the hushed voice inside your head.'

Isabelle listened eagerly to Whisper's description of all the great things that she would be learning on Aydagar. Something called *Life Secrets*, which were just as important as all the subjects she was already studying at school. Knowledge that could change the way Isabelle thought about herself and help her make her dreams come true.

'The Life Secrets are revealed to only those who seek them out,' Whisper said.

'So, you can only learn these secrets on Aydagar?' Isabelle asked.

'Not at all! Our life experiences usually teach us some of these secrets. But, believe it or not, there are actually many grown-ups who don't know about them.'

'Really. How come?' asked Isabelle.

'There are many reasons,' said Whisper, 'but mostly it's because people let their life just happen to them. They grow older, without ever questioning or learning from the lessons that life gives them.'

'But I'm only twelve years old,' Isabelle said.

'That's plenty old enough,' replied Whisper. 'The earlier you learn these secrets, the better.'

Taking a deep breath, Whisper looked deep into Isabelle's eyes.

'Are you ready to be a GeeBee?' she said.

'A GeeBee – that sounds funny,' said Isabelle.

'Anyone choosing to go to Aydagar and learn about the incredible powers of their mind is called a Great Budding Explorer, or GeeBee for short.'

Whisper continued to explain that just as a tiny bud unfurls its petals and bursts into bloom, so a GeeBee would blossom by learning all the secrets that Aydagar had to show them.

'You'll learn how to start taking charge of your life,'

said Whisper.

'You mean like being my own boss?' said Isabelle.

Whisper nodded and chuckled gently.

Tinkle – tinkle - ting-a-ling.

'*Whoaa,*' said Isabelle, more loudly than intended.

Whenever she couldn't find the right words, she would express herself with colourful sounds instead. Although people would often laugh, Isabelle's message was always loud and clear.

'It's up to you, Izzy. Are you ready to do this?

'Well, I suppose so,' said Isabelle.

Her own hesitant reply caught her off guard: she wanted to go, but was she good enough to face up to this challenge? Isabelle hated the self-doubt, but didn't know how to stop it creeping into her mind.

Knowing Isabelle better than anyone in the whole wide world, Whisper had expected such a reaction. She reassured her that she, like everyone else, had talents, abilities and strengths; and that it was often a matter of knowledge and having life experiences, until she discovered what they were.

'It's just that often we're unaware of our abilities because they're buried deep within us like a treasure trove, waiting to be discovered,' said Whisper. 'Question is, are you ready to explore your greatness?'

Isabelle's face lit up instantly.

'Yes!' she said, with a new feeling of confidence.

She bent forward and tried to hug Whisper, but her arms just went right through her body.

'Oh, I forgot, you're invisible,' said Isabelle, backing away from her translucent twin.

The girls talked in whispers for a while longer. They had just met; at least, it partly seemed that way to Isabelle. Yet she felt like she had known Whisper all her life.

'Any final questions?'

'Can I, I mean, is it okay if my friends come with me?' said Isabelle.

'I don't see why not,' was Whisper's cheery response.

With that matter sorted, Whisper began to explain what would happen from this point onward. She spoke of a secret passageway next to the fireplace in the school's main entrance hall, which would lead them down to an underground river.

'Once you get there, Captain Mentor will be waiting to take you to Aydagar.'

'What do you mean, *you*?' said Isabelle, panicked. 'You'll be with me, won't you?'

Whisper reassured Isabelle that even though she wouldn't be able to see her, she would always sense Whisper's presence within her and all around her.

'You'll feel me in the breeze, in the rays of light that touch your face and in the nature that lives and breathes all around you.'

'I am you and you are me,' Isabelle replayed Whisper's words in her head.

'That's right, and always remember, I am a reflection of everything that is in you and so, am always with you.'

Whisper blew her an invisible kiss from her fingertips and with a sudden blusterous whooshing sound, disappeared back to Isabelle's inner world.

'Aww,' Isabelle's gasped in astonishment.

Before she could help it, she let out a little cry, then clamped both hands over her mouth to stop any more noise from coming out. Isabelle got up to her knees slowly and looked out of the window into the darkness, her heart pounding in her ears.

'Whisper?' she hissed out softly.

For a moment, she heard nothing and wondered if she'd imagined the whole thing. Then came the sound of a voice she knew well.

'Is that you Izzy?'

Akira stuck her head around the curtain. She flicked back her straight, black hair off her chubby face and arched her eyebrows, waiting for an answer.

'Let me see,' said another voice, right behind her.

Holly peeked behind the curtain, smiling and showing off her perfectly straight white teeth.

'Hatched your plan of escape yet?' she said, with a sly smile.

As she tied her long hair up in a ponytail, Isabelle couldn't help but admire her friend's delicate, slightly upturned nose, freckled face and heavenly strawberry-blonde hair.

'What are you doing?' said Akira.

'You won't believe what just happened,' said Isabelle, making room on the wide windowsill.

'Try me.'

Akira climbed up and plopped herself down clumsily opposite Isabelle. Holly, who was slimmer and at least three inches taller, decided there wasn't enough room for her as well, so she remained standing with the curtains pulled around her back, like a velvety cape.

Holly and Akira listened as Isabelle explained all that had happened, since lights out. She talked excitedly and incessantly without hardly taking a breath.

'*Wow*, so what are you going to do?' said Holly.

'It's not what she's going to do. It's what we're all going to do,' said Akira.

'You mean …' said Isabelle.

'Well, we either do it together or nobody does it at all,' said Akira, in her usual matter-of-fact way.

What Akira lacked in height, she made up for with gumption and spirit. But it was her imposing manner and expression, being able to say precisely what she thought at the right time, which made Akira stand out from the crowd. It was this quality that impressed Isabelle above all about her friend.

'I'm in,' said Holly.

She held her hand out, wiggled her fingers and made a fist.

'It's a done deal then,' said Akira.

They laughed as they fist-bumped, hardly able to contain their excitement at the thought of taking this challenge together.

In record time the girls fumbled around their belongings in the dark, putting on and gathering whatever each one thought might be useful. They had to be quiet and they had to be quick.

'You can't be serious, Akira!' Holly said, in a loud whisper.

'Well, someone has to represent the school,' was Akira's quiet, but sharp reply.

She was wearing her school uniform; navy pleated skirt, white shirt, striped tie, knee socks, and a navy padded waistcoat. It was the only natural thing for Akira to do; she was very academic and loved her boarding school.

'Suit yourself then,' said Holly.

She had changed into her tracksuit and trainers and started to do some stretching exercises while she was waiting.

Isabelle grabbed her backpack, took out her school books, and replaced them with things she thought might be useful on their journey. She put in a pocket torch, mini binoculars, a Swiss army-knife, some cereal bars, plus some other things.

'I guess that's it,' she said, putting on her short boots and zipping up the front of her sweatshirt.

'Ready or not, let's go,' said Akira.

The girls gave each other one final look of determination and tiptoed quietly towards the door. An expert by now at avoiding creaky floorboards, Isabelle took the lead. She popped her head out of the dorm door and, when she was sure the coast was clear, started walking down the corridor, keeping her back as near the wall as possible.

Akira and Holly followed as closely as they could, creeping down the wide stone staircase and into the grand entrance hall of the school. Their hearts beat wildly as they stood in front of the grand fireplace, uncertain of their next move.

'I think this must be …' Isabelle said, just about to point out something.

'What's going on?'

The husky voice came from nowhere and made them jump. Standing silent for a minute, the girls shot each other a quick, worried sideways glance of concern.

'*Uh oh,*' said Isabelle, and grimaced.

She knew the punishment for sneaking off the school grounds.

They turned round slowly, expecting a teacher. But instead, they saw Jack and Finn who had come over from the boys' side, of the school.

'Oh, it's only you.'

Holly lolled her tongue out and breathed a sigh of relief.

'Don't you ever do that again,' Akira told Jack through gritted teeth. 'Never, never, understand?'

'*Pfft,* what, never?' said Jack, sarcastically.

Hands on hips in a stance of arrogance, Akira snarled back at him.

'Never.'

'Gosh, you scared us,' said Holly.

'Sorry,' said Finn, sheepishly.

He blushed until his face was almost the colour of his hair, even making the spray of freckles that covered his cheeks and nose stand out.

'What are you doing here?' Akira demanded.

'We live here too, you know,' said Jack.

'Yes, but you're supposed to be in the boy's west wing.'

'And you're supposed to be in the east wing, with the girls,' said Jack.

He smiled, his cockiness melting into a relaxed confidence.

'Yes but, why are you here - now?' said Isabelle.

'If you must know, we were ghost hunting,' said Jack.

Wigmore Abbey hadn't always been a boarding school. Before that, it was a sanatorium for people suffering from tuberculosis. The building was believed to be haunted by the ghosts of those who didn't realise they were dead. Jack and Finn were looking for the building's best-known ghost, the Black Count of Wigmore.

'This spot here, is where he usually appears,' whispered Finn. 'For a moment, we thought you were him.'

'An honest mistake to make in the dark,' said Jack, throwing his shoulders back and standing up straight.

Jack was the tallest of the group and rather gangly, with deep-set dark eyes and a frizzy mass of dark hair. He was full of pranks and practical jokes that were usually harmless, but could sometimes lead to people getting very hurt.

'Were you going to zap the ghosts dressed like that?' said Akira.

She tutted as she pointed to Finn's clothes. He was dressed

in full cricket kit; batting leg pads, leather gloves and a helmet with the face shield lifted up over his face. Without saying a word, Finn pushed his round thin-rimmed glasses further up his nose and quickly put his bat into a long, narrow bag and swung it over his shoulder.

'We've got this as well,' said Jack, whipping out a small slingshot from his back pocket.

'Oh, please,' said Akira, sarcastically.

'Just ignore her,' Jack said.

He gave his friend a playful, but sharp jab in the ribs. Even though Finn was stocky and quite well-padded, he let out a gasp - *'ahhh'* - and buckled slightly.

Isabelle didn't know Finn well, but she felt sorry for him. It was so obvious that he was Jack's "yes" person, always agreeing with him and doing his dirty work. In many ways, Finn reminded Isabelle of herself.

'What'ya doing here anyway?' said Jack. 'Are you planning something? What is it?'

'Shall we tell them?' Isabelle looked at Akira.

'Hm-m-m,' she said, crossing her arms across her chest, acting as if she was somehow in charge.

Holly on the other hand, who was always so eager to please anyone said, 'Yes, let's.'

'Whisper said anyone could come,' said Isabelle.

'Go on then,' said Jack.

'Okay, you can tell them,' said Akira.

Isabelle eagerly began relating what had happened to her on the windowsill, and what they intended to do. It didn't take much persuading to get the boys excited about joining them.

'I wouldn't miss this chance for the world,' said Jack. 'We're in.'

He yanked Finn by the t-shirt and made a beeline for the secret oak panel to the right of the fireplace. After some time spent fumbling around, Jack felt something like a cut in the wood and pressed it. There was a click sound, like a latch being opened, followed by a creak and a long silence.

The five of them stared blankly as the full-length wooden panel slowly opened inwards, revealing a shadowy opening. For a few brief moments, they all huddled around the entrance, wondering what lay beyond the thick wall of cobwebs.

'Ladies first,' said Jack.

'*Huh*, only when it suits you,' Akira said.

'I was only being polite.'

'Sure, you were,' Akira said, screwing up her eyes.

'It's okay, I'll go,' said Isabelle.

After rummaging in her backpack for her pocket torch, she gingerly pushed the cobwebs to the side with the back of her hand, cringing as the strands stuck to her fingers and hoodie

'*Ugh*,' she said.

She tried to brush them away, but the sticky threads seemed to cling tighter the more she flayed her arms in the air.

'Are you okay?' said Holly,

'Yeah, I think so,' said Isabelle.

Calming herself with deep breaths, she used the dim light of her torch to peer into the pitch-black passage. Taking only a few steps forward, a pungent, earthy smell hit Isabelle, and she instinctively wrinkled her nose in disgust.

'*Ewww*, it stinks in here,' she said, wafting her hand in front of her face.

'It smells like pee,' said Holly.

'Maybe this wasn't such a good idea after all,' said Akira.

'We're not turning back now,' said Jack, prodding Akira in

the back.

'Get off,' said Akira, swinging round to take a swipe at Jack.

'Just move,' said Jack.

'If you ever touch me again, it'll be the last thing you do,' said Akira.

'Give it a break, you two,' said Holly.

The passage was narrow, and the tiny light of the torch only reached a few feet in front of them. It soon gave way to a spiral stone staircase. Isabelle pointed her torch downwards, and all they could see were steps winding down into darkness.

'I guess we go down,' said Finn.

'Guess so,' said Isabelle.

'Or we could come back another day,' Akira started to say.

'Maybe you might want to, but we're going down,' said Jack.

Grabbing Isabelle's torch, Jack took the lead, and the group slowly made their way down the stairwell, which went down and down, and down. Until finally, it opened up into a long tunnel carved into the rock.

'It's so stuffy down here,' said Holly.

'And difficult to breathe,' said Akira.

'Just hold your breath, like forever,' Jack said jokingly.

'Oh ha-ha-ha,' Akira snarled.

'Come on, let's go,' said Isabelle.

The group slowly groped their way along the unfamiliar, damp passageway, which twisted to the right and left at intervals.

'Are you sure it's not some kind of labyrinth,' said Akira, holding onto Isabelle's backpack.

'I'm not sure of anything,' said Isabelle.

Then, they heard the faint sound of rushing water. It got louder and louder the further they walked, and within two hundred feet or so, they went around a final bend.

'Look, there's a light,' said Isabelle.

'Where's it coming from?' said Finn.

'It must be an opening.'

'Well, there's only one way to find out,' said Jack.

They all pushed forward, hurrying one behind the other until the tunnel led them to an underground river.

'*Whoaa,*' Finn and Isabelle exclaimed together.

For a split second, they all froze, mouths gaping open as they stared at a huge vessel moored in front of them. It must have been the strangest yacht they'd ever seen; its very unconventional prow tapering to a point that jutted out from the rest of the ship.

'It's like a swordfish,' said Jack, rushing to the front of the vessel.

'Maybe it's a spaceship,' said Holly.

'A spaceship on water,' said Akira, giving her friend a slightly condescending look.

Holly just giggled, feeling a little embarrassed.

'Well, it does look like something from the future,' said Finn.

'It actually looks like that warship. You know, the one the ancient Greeks had. What was it called?' asked Jack.

His question was answered immediately by Akira.

'A trireme.'

Akira was not only smart, but was known at school as a walking encyclopaedia about almost everything. And she didn't need much persuading to talk about what she knew.

'They were also known as the dark-eyed ships.'

Two polished painted marble plaques were positioned on either side of the prow, each depicting an eye. Below it was painted the word *Discovery*.

A loud coughing sound, followed by a deep, booming voice

came from the boat.

'Are there any GeeBees here?'

Someone was coming up on deck from below, and he looked very important. Within seconds, a tall man, in a tightly fitting black, linen waistcoat with decorative metal buttons arrived on deck. Looking at a gold pocket watch he said, 'It's about time. I am Captain Andronicus Mentor.'

'Is he a pirate?' said Jack under his breath.

'He sort of looks like one,' said Holly.

'No, he doesn't,' said Akira, sharply. 'He's too clean and smart to be a pirate.'

'No, it's the man that Whisper talked about,' said Isabelle.

The Captain had a well-trimmed black moustache and beard, with greying, long hair that swept back from his brow, tied in a ponytail. Together with the mustard-coloured sash around his waist, black waistcoat, and boots, he did somehow resemble a character out of a buccaneer story.

'Not a pirate my friends, just a passionate explorer of life,' said the Captain.

He pressed a button that lowered a gangplank into position, so that they could all come aboard.

'Well, don't just stand there,' he said.

His emerald-green eyes sparkled with friendliness as he smiled at them all.

Filled with excitement, all five explorers sprang aboard, where the Captain greeted them one by one with a handshake and a firm slap on the back.

'Let's commence your journey of self-discovery,' he said, leading them onto the expansive, state-of-the-art bridge deck.

Isabelle paused, thinking back to Whisper and the moment she agreed to take on this challenge. A challenge that she was now carrying into this sea vessel like an unopened gift, and one that would most likely change her life forever.

POWER COAST

3

KIRIARHOS NOUS
*
MASTER MIND

The Captain's bridge sat on top of the primary hull and, like the exterior of the sailboat, looked like something out of a sci-fi film. The entrance opened up into a control room that was sleek and modern in design, with curved maple wood fittings blending in exquisitely with its pure white surroundings.

Captain Mentor's leather chair was in the centre of the room, directly in front of the helm console station from where navigation control was carried out. Five chairs, slightly smaller in size than the Captain's, surrounded the central console.

'Buckle up,' said the Captain.

Safety belts were installed at each seat position and each chair was securely fastened by means of bolts to the floor.

'You bet,' said Finn, with a smile on his face.

He rushed and sat himself down in a chair to the right of the Captain.

'This is going to be fun,' said Holly, clapping her

hands eagerly.

'I'm not so sure about that,' mumbled Akira.

'*Huh*, too bad for you then,' said Jack.

Two minutes later they were all strapped in their seats and the Captain started pressing various buttons on a tiny status display on his armrest.

'Aurora, let's get the show on the road.'

Before anyone had time to work out who Aurora was, the lights on the glass covered control panel in front of them suddenly came to life, responding with a slightly muffled, digital voice.

'Yes, Captain.'

'Plot the course for Aydagar,' said Captain Mentor, touching the screen in front of him.

'Aye, aye, Captain,' responded Aurora.

Metal screens on the outside of the forward bulkhead started to rise upwards like shutters. This revealed a massive panoramic widescreen that wrapped entirely around to the sides of the vessel.

The Discovery broke from her anchors and pushed out of the mouth of the cave, soon heeling over as the strong south wind caught her sails. The yacht sped through the water as the winds strengthened and, before long, the coastline of their familiar world slowly disappeared from view.

'I get the feeling that we're sailing into the other side of nowhere,' Holly whispered into Isabelle's ear.

'Me, too. But we just have to trust him.'

Akira was equally unsure how they would reach their destination, or if it actually existed.

'So, where exactly is this Aydagar?'

'*Ahh,* Aydagar lies far beyond the Northern isles,' he

answered, slowly and knowingly.

'How come I've never heard of it, or the Northern isles before?' said Akira.

'Just because you haven't heard of something, doesn't mean it's not there.'

The Captain looked at Akira expectantly and winked.

As hours passed and they were well out into open waters, the wind became wilder, the sea grew fiercer, and everyone on board became increasingly nervous. The Discovery ploughed on, rising and plunging, rising and plunging over each wave. Showers of sea-spray covered the entire glass windscreen in front of them, going up as high as the mast.

'This boat must be water-tight,' said Holly.

She had to almost shout in order to be heard.

'I just hope we don't get smashed to pieces,' said Akira, gripping the arms of her chair.

'We're gonna be okay, right?' said Isabelle, looking at the Captain for reassurance.

Captain M looked up at the dark, menacing clouds above them and answered calmly, 'You're all quite safe. Everything is as it should ...'

But before he had finished the sentence, his voice was wiped out by the reverberating sound of an enormous thunderclap. A split second later, the sky opened up with a brilliant flash of lighting and the rain started pouring down like a heavy black curtain all around them.

It seemed that the storm would continue forever until, suddenly, the Discovery shuddered and started to lean to one side.

'Lower the sails.'

Aurora automatically obeyed the Captain's command.

The sails folded and together with the mast, retracted like a kaleidoscope into the main body of the boat.

'What's going on?' said Isabelle, clenching the consul for support.

'Hold on, we'll be going through the Strovilos Vortex any moment now,' the Captain called out.

'Vortex!' called out Akira.

Everyone had the same panicky look on their faces. It was the first time they had ever heard of such a phenomenon and yet now, they were being helplessly sucked into its epicentre. It was all happening so quickly and, as everyone strained to understand what was going on, the sea suddenly ripped wide open, forcing the Discovery to tilt sideways.

'We're going down,' screamed Holly.

'I can't swim, I'm going to drown,' cried Akira.

'Where are we going to end up?' asked Finn.

'The bottom of the ocean,' said Jack, inwardly afraid, but outwardly brave.

'Oh nooo,' Isabelle let out a muffled scream.

'Just hold on tight,' called out the Captain.

Their whimpering cries and screams were drowned out by the howling roar of the giant whirlpool. Round and round the Discovery went, shaking and creaking as if it were on the point of breaking in two.

Then, like water draining away down a plughole, the vessel and everyone on board instantaneously vanished off the radar of the earthly realm.

Crazy colourful patterns and fuzzy images started to fill everyone's thoughts as they were being sucked down into the spinning vortex. Before long, the five GeeBees slipped into a blurred unconsciousness and into nothingness; into an infinite space, where they simply became nobody, nothing, in no time.

How long they remained in this unconscious state can never be told. But the spinning did eventually slow down, and once again everything was calm. The Discovery was rocking gently, with slow creaking noises on a tranquil sea.

The hypnotic sound of water lapping against the sides of the ship's hull woke the GeeBees from what could only be described as a deep sleep.

'Awww,' Holly yawned loudly.

'Are we there yet?' asked Isabelle, forcing her limp body to an upright position.

Akira rubbed her heavy eyelids, trying to pry them open.

'Are we still under water?'

'Don't think so,' said Finn, squinting at the sunlight coming in through the large windscreen.

It took some time to rouse them all but once they were properly awake, the Captain proceeded to tell them that they had arrived at their destination.

'We're alive,' Akira said for the fourth time. 'I mean, we went through a vortex and came out alive.'

'It's so crazy, and fantastic,' said Finn.

'I don't remember anything. Everything went fuzzy,' said Isabelle.

'All I remember is the boat tilting,' said Jack.

'I still can't believe we're really here,' said Isabelle.

'Me, neither,' said Holly, giggling nervously.

Her high-pitched giggles always ended in a cute little snort, which made everyone laugh when they heard it. On purpose, Jack snorted with laughter and said, 'Miss Piggy.'

'Ha, ha,' she responded, sticking the tip of her tongue out at him.

All of a sudden, the Captain sprung out of his chair and walked purposefully over to the hatch door. As he opened it, the salty air of the sea flooded the cabin, as did a louder sound of water sloshing against the Discovery.

When he signalled for everyone to go out, Finn took off like a shot, disappearing through the open door as though he was afraid it might close again. He scampered up the steps as fast as he could onto the deck of the sailboat.

'Come on you lot, look at this,' he called out.

A sudden rush of excitement swept everyone off their feet and onto the ship's deck. They all stood there, not speaking, scanning their new surroundings.

'I think it is the most beautiful place I have ever been to,' sighed Isabelle.

'Is this really Aydagar?' Holly asked.

'The one and only,' replied the Captain, with a beaming smile.

The scene before them looked like a water colour painting of an exotic, untouched land. Standing prominently in the foreground was a thick line of tall coconut palms running the length of a long white, sandy beach.

In the far background, two prominent rock formations jutted out spectacularly into the air, looming over the island like two silent masters. And with a few touches of rocky-grey terrain, thick green forests and white fluffy clouds in a diluted blue sky, the dreamy canvas was complete.

'Let's get the exploration moving,' said Captain Mentor, climbing down into a dinghy.

As the group rowed to shore, dozens of seagulls circled above them, screeching and squabbling with each other.

'Do you think they're trying to say something,' said Jack.

'They're probably telling us to go home,' said Akira.

She couldn't believe that they had made it through the Strovilos Vortex and was almost sorry she had agreed to come on this adventure.

'Maybe, they're just saying hello,' said Isabelle.

'Whatever, they're just really annoying,' Jack said, covering his ears.

The Captain reached under his legs, took out a tin box of sandwich bags and handed them around.

'Yum, breakfast!' said Finn, rubbing his stomach.

'I'm starving,' said Jack as he tucked in.

They all munched away quite happily, and soon enough the dinghy reached shore, gliding silently to a stop in the white sand. Jumping out of the boat the five explorers wandered along the beach, throwing pebbles into the sea, laughing at who could make the biggest splash.

Finn picked up a huge spiky conch-like shell and turned it upside down to see what was inside. Instantly, a crustaceous creature, measuring no less than five inches jumped out of the shell. It had stalk eyes, at least ten jointed legs, a huge claw and a tail that was structured like a scorpion's.

'Aggh,' he yelled, and tossed the shell into the air.

What he had not realised was that the whole beach was riddled with these creatures hiding under every shell. Then, as if some electric signal had been given off, hundreds and hundreds of these crab-like creatures started scurrying to and fro on the beach. Some crawled slowly under the weight of their shells whilst others ditched them, snapping their huge single claw in the air as they ran.

'Ugh, they're so ugly,' said Akira, tiptoeing carefully, in case she trod on one.

'Look at them go!' said Jack.

He tried his best to grab one, but it was too fast, and he ended up tumbling into the soft sand empty-handed.

'Grab it from behind,' Finn called out.

'Careful, it'll chop your finger off,' said Holly.

Jack scooped up a handful of sand and watched it run through his fingers.

'It looks and feels like sand,' he said, 'but it's got all these shiny bits.'

He picked up another handful and as he let it sift through his fingers, myriads of shiny black and crystal grains sparkling in the sun. He had never seen anything quite like this before.

'Are those stars,' said Akira, pointing skywards.

'What, during the day?' said Isabelle.

'That can't be right,' said Finn.

And yet overhead, the daytime sky was sprinkled with yellow twinkling stars.

'This place is weird,' said Holly.

'It's sort of the same as home …' Isabelle started.

'But so different,' Akira said.

'Exactly!'

'Come on, let's get started,' Captain Mentor called out.

He headed inland, into a dense wall of jungle. After around ten minutes or so of walking, the Captain stopped at a huge tree and patted the twisted, wrinkled trunk. Nestled up in its higher branches, almost deep inside the trunk itself, was an old tree house. A rope ladder dangled from a branch. It looked old but sturdy enough.

'Up you go,' he said.

Everyone's eyes widened and their mouths hung open as they looked up at the towering tree. Except for Holly. She leapt onto the second rung without a second thought and quickly scaled the ladder, almost as fast as if she was climbing a staircase. She looked down at her friends from a platform and said, 'It's easy peasy.'

'Easy for you maybe,' said Akira.

Nothing irritated Akira more than arduous physical activity. Except for Jack, that is. She found him even more irritating.

'My turn next, I don't want Akira's fat bum in my face,' said Jack.

'Get lost,' she retorted, and stuck her tongue out at him.

By the time everyone made their way up, Holly had already crept inside and was inspecting every nook and cranny. The tree house was comprised of a single rectangular room with two large windows. Solid bamboo poles with overlapping layers of closely-knit canes ran three feet above their heads. A hanging lantern swung backwards and forwards in the gentle breeze. At the far end of the room stood a bookshelf containing stacks of parchments, scrolls, and books of every imaginable shape and size.

The girls made themselves comfortable on the well-worn patchwork sofa in the middle of the room, and Finn sat on one of the arms. Jack lurked behind the girls menacingly, wiggling his finger in the air at very close range to their heads.

'Get lost Jack,' Akira said, twisting her head around and glaring at him.

'Not touching you,' said Jack, annoyingly.

The Captain walked over to a large upright barrel by the door and picked up two walnuts from a bowl. He skilfully played with them in his huge hands.

'Is that our breakfast, Captain M?' said Jack, jokingly.

'His name is Captain Mentor,' said Akira.

42

She spoke through gritted teeth, as she often did when she talked to Jack.

'Whatever,' replied Jack, flicking her hair from behind.

'I actually like the sound of that. Captain M it is then,' Captain Mentor replied, jovially.

Jack smiled like a little kid, rubbed his hands together and made an *'ah-ha'* sound by the side of Akira's ear.

The Captain put the walnuts into his pocket and walked to a chest in the corner of the room. He bent down, unlocked it with a key kept on a chain hanging around his neck, then pulled out a large scroll. On it was printed a huge map.

'This, my friends, is Aydagar.'

The island was clearly divided into three very different regions. Running along the south-eastern part of the island was the Power Coast, where they had dropped anchor. Situated in the northern-central region were two huge rock pinnacles called the Avaton Towers.

'And due west are the Monster Caves,' he said, with a spooky tone in his voice.

'Monster Caves!'

Akira always seemed to be more startled than the others.

'That's where you'll meet your match,' Jack joked.

He yanked a tuft of Akira's hair from behind.

'Cut it out, Jack.'

Akira swung around and tried to thump Jack, but missed as he darted backwards out of her reach.

Captain M cleared his throat loudly and continued his explanation; with his help, the GeeBees would explore the whole island, collecting nine Life Secrets. Three from the Power Coast, three from the Monster Caves, and finally, three from the Avaton Towers.

'As well as nine corresponding golden tokens,' he said.

He tapped his forefinger on the Power Coast, their current position.

'And now, for the first Life Secret.'

He put the map down on the table and took both walnuts out of his pocket with his left hand. Closing his eyes tight, he started making the most peculiar movement with his right hand. With his fist closed, he moved his hand in a quick, anti-clockwise circular motion over his open left palm. It was almost as if he was winding in a fishing reel.

Ten, twenty, thirty seconds passed. There was no way of knowing what the Captain was doing. But he was clearly mulling something very important over in his head. Perhaps he was casting some kind of spell?

Then he suddenly stopped, opened his eyes, and pressed the walnuts against each other, using all the force he could muster. There was a cracking sound as the hinge of the shells gave way.

'Master Mind,' he said, with great gusto.

The Captain slowly and carefully removed the thick outer shell to reveal the pulpy inner nut.

'Our skull is like this hard, outer shell,' he said.

He tipped the shell fragments onto the table and placed its contents onto his open palm.

'And this is just like our brain,' he continued.

With its surface covered in little wrinkles and folds, the walnut really did look very much like a human brain. It was formed in two halves, and each side was joined together in the middle.

'It's quite soft,' said Holly, reaching out to poke the nut.

'And tasty,' said Jack.

Even the faint smell of the walnut reminded him that he

44

was still hungry.

'Now, here is the left and right hemisphere, the upper and lower cerebellum,' the Captain continued, pointing to different areas of the walnut.

A rush of eagerness ran through Finn and he couldn't help but interrupt.

'Different parts of the brain have different functions, and there are a lot of parts whose uses we don't understand.'

'That's right, Finn,' responded the Captain.

Finn was no artist or musician, but he had a passion for nature, science and science fiction. His father worked in the field of biomedical research and always encouraged Finn's interests, supplying him with books and magazines to read on all sorts of such subjects.

'The science nerd has spoken,' laughed Jack.

'Well, at least he uses his brain before he talks,' snarled Akira.

'Just ignore them,' Holly told the Captain. 'They're always falling out over something.'

Akira's tendency to be pushy, stubborn, and impatient nearly always clashed with Jack's arrogance and inclination to belittle those around him. They both believed they were always right, and even though their fighting and bickering never changed a thing, they continued to do so incessantly.

The Captain once again cleared his throat loudly to attract everyone's attention.

'Do you want to discover how you can take charge and start becoming the leader of your life?'

There was a strained silence before he spoke again.

'So, the first step is to begin to understand about the extraordinary power of your mind.'

'Well, I for one want to know,' Isabelle said.

'That's why we're here, isn't it?' Akira said.

She turned around and gave Jack a growling sound.

A gust of wind suddenly rocked the tree house, causing the old timber frame to creak eerily. As it died down, all that was left in the air was the ghostly sound of hissing voices; talking over each other and repeating certain words in a strange language.

'What was that?' gasped Holly

'Did you hear that?' said Akira.

'Yes, I did,' said Finn.

'What was it?' repeated Holly.

She clung onto Isabelle's and Akira's arms, giggling nervously.

'The island's winds can sometimes play funny tricks,' said the Captain, smiling. 'And often there is a message to be heard.'

Trick or no trick, no one dared speak. So, the Captain continued.

'Your brain is probably the most complex structure in the known universe,' he said. 'No other brain in the animal kingdom is so ingenious.'

He propped himself on the edge of the table, and folded his arms with a contented sigh.

'Your mind is like a supercomputer, and it's made up of two parts; your conscious and subconscious,' he continued.

The conscious mind, he explained to them, was the part that they were using to listen to him.

'You mean, now that we're thinking about everything you're telling us?' said Akira.

'That's right,' he said. 'But that's only a tiny part of your mind; it's just the tip of the iceberg.'

'The biggest part of the iceberg is under the water,' said Finn.

'Exactly so,' said the Captain. 'And in the same way, the

biggest part of the mind is the subconscious. It's the part you're not aware of.'

'So, what does it do?' said Isabelle.

'*Ahh*, well, your subconscious mind helps you function as a human being,' replied the Captain. 'And it does some pretty amazing things.'

'Like what?' asked Jack.

'First of all, it controls all your bodily functions,' the Captain said. 'Like sending the signals to make your heart beat, your lungs breathe and your eyes blink.'

'I know, I know …' said Finn. 'I know that our hearts beat around one hundred and fifteen thousand times a day?'

'Seriously, why would anyone know something like that?' said Jack, screwing up his face.

The Captain smiled at Finn, giving him a quick wink.

'And yet, it is very relevant to what we are talking about, Jack,' said the Captain. 'Your subconscious mind is like a huge filing cabinet that stores all your memories, habits and automatic responses. It never sleeps, always processing something.'

Captain M paused for a moment, long enough for his words to sink in.

'All the information about everything you have ever experienced in your lives up to now is stored there.'

'Wow,' gasped Holly.

'That's a pretty big filing cabinet,' said Akira.

The Captain nodded and smiled.

'That's incredible,' said Isabelle.

'So, the mind is actually just like a computer,' said Jack.

'Yes, Jack, it certainly is. In fact, the mind is very much like the Discovery. I am the Captain and therefore …'

'Like the conscious mind,' said Akira.

'Exactly. I make all the decisions and give all the orders.'

'So, that means the subconscious is just like the control centre of the Discovery,' said Finn.

'You mean Aurora,' said Isabelle.

'Yes, Aurora does the rest,' said the Captain.

'Like when it lowered the sails and the mast,' said Jack.

The Captain smiled and nodded, happy that the explorers had cottoned on so quickly to the First Secret.

'Just like a computer software programme,' added Jack.

'You see, it's all about teamwork. With your Captain conscious mind, you think about what it is that you want, and then your Aurora subconscious mind uses its amazing resources to work on helping you achieve whatever it is that you desire.'

Digging into his breast pocket, the Captain pulled out a rather old looking leather pouch and jingled it up and down.

'Is that money in there?' asked Holly.

'It's the tokens I mentioned earlier. One for each Life Secret.'

Opening the pouch, Captain M rummaged around and pulled out a token the size of a two-penny coin. One side bore the image of a brain and on the other the inscription, Master Mind.

The Captain flipped the golden token into the air, where it twisted and turned until he finally caught it in his left hand. Walking over to Isabelle, he placed the token in her hand.

'Why me?' she said, staring at the token in disbelief.

'Yeah, why her?' asked Jack, almost spitefully.

'Were it not for Izzy, none of you would be here. It is therefore only fitting that she receives the first token,' replied the Captain.

Isabelle felt her cheeks flush with a mixture of pride and embarrassment.

The GeeBees all took it in turn to examine the token and, as Akira held it in her hand, she read some words running around its perimeter.

'Kiriarhos Nous,' she said, her mouth gaping wide open.

These words were from a language that she had studied for a couple of years.

'That's Greek … for Master Mind.'

Ancient Greek was a compulsory lesson at school, and was a subject at which Akira particularly excelled. So much so that she rarely made errors in her cases or tenses.

'Yes, Akira, indeed it is,' replied the Captain. 'But here on Aydagar, we refer to our language as Hellenic.'

'That's impossible,' Akira exclaimed.

The Captain smiled a wry smile.

'There is no such thing as impossible, Akira. Everything is *effiktable*.'

'Effik what?' said Jack.

'Effiktable! It's a word that I made up,' said the Captain. 'From the Hellenic word "effikto", which means possible, plus an English ending.'

The corners of his mouth lifted, and he burst into laughter.

'Anything is eff - ik - table,' Isabelle said slowly.

'That sounds funny, but it's kind'ov catchy,' Holly said.

They all looked at each other and laughed, repeating the word over and over again like a chant, as if they were trying to get the right accent.

'Effiktable, effiktable, effiktable!'

And now, with the first secret revealed, it was a secret no more, but rather knowledge that would help the GeeBees on their journey of self-discovery.

Wasting no time, they all left the tree house and followed

the Captain as he made his way deeper into the jungle. No-one knew where they were being taken, nor could they be sure about what lay ahead. But the promise of untold secrets filled them with a curious mixture of apprehension and exhilaration, driving them forwards like an invisible force.

They could all feel it.

4

SKEPSEIS KARDIAS
*
HEART THOUGHTS

Heading westwards, the explorers took a narrow path that led around the bay, with the sea on their left and cliffs overhanging them on the right. The early morning quiet was interrupted only by the swish of their strides as they walked, and the occasional hooting sound in the far distance.

'All in all, you will see the rise and fall of the golden sun and silver moon three times,' the Captain told them.

'You mean we're here for three days?' said Akira.

'And three nights – *yay*,' said Isabelle.

She clenched her right fist and pulled her forearm back in a sign of triumph. Her escape plan had not only worked, but had turned out better than she could have ever imagined.

Now, no-one would be able to find her for three whole days and nights.

'I've never been away from home on my own before,' said Holly.

'But, you're not on your own,' said Jack.

'I meant to say ...' said Holly, pausing for a moment. 'Actually, I don't know what I meant to say.'

She grinned at Jack, feeling embarrassed. He tutted and rolled his eyes to show what an idiot he thought she was.

'Do you really like making people feel so little?' Akira asked him.

Jack snorted and looked down his nose at her.

Huge trees towered above them, so tall they blocked out most of the sunlight.

'This is so amazing, I can't believe we're doing this,' said Isabelle.

'I've walked with dad so many times in forests, but never seen anything like this in my life,' said Finn.

'It's awesome,' said Holly.

Walking slowly along the winding trail through the deep jungle, they were all surprised at the different species of ferns and exotic plants growing all around them. Even above their heads, pretty colourful orchids grew wildly on the smaller branches and twigs of the trees. Everything looked so beautiful in the soft, green light.

When the Captain took out his knife to cut away some thick, rubbery leaves blocking their way, a cloud of tiny buzzing objects filled the air around them.

'Gnats!' Akira said, as they came towards her.

'They're bigger, more like mozzies,' said Finn.

'Look at those long stings,' Jack said, as the flying insects flitted around his eyes.

'D'ya think they're a pre-historic species,' said Finn.

'Who cares?' said Jack.

He kept on clapping his hands together, trying to squish or

at least trap them.

'*Ouch*, it got me,' said Holly, swatting a bug on her cheek.

'*Owww*,' that was like a pin prick,' said Jack, looking in between his fingers.

'Are they poisonous?' said Holly.

'Don't worry, they might just leave you scratching for a while,' said the Captain.

The insects hung in the air around them, rising and falling, and no matter how many times everyone tried to swat them away, they kept on coming back.

'What should we do – *oww*,' said Akira.

'*Fttt, fttt*,' Isabelle spat out repeatedly as a foul, bitter taste filled her mouth. 'It flew into my mouth.'

She wiped her tongue vigorously with the sleeve of her sweatshirt.

'Keep on moving, they'll stop soon enough,' said the Captain.

In the end, the swirling mass of gnats didn't stay put as the Captain had predicted, and for about half an hour the explorers walked on, chatting about this and that. Suddenly, a rustling sound, followed by a scurry in the bushes, made them all jump.

Without warning, a group of copper red monkeys burst out of the bushes, zipping past them and straight up a tree. Scarcely bigger than a squirrel, the tiny creatures frantically jumped from branch to branch, squabbling and performing tricks; stopping for only a moment to nibble on some purple fruit.

'What are they eating?' said Finn.

'Whatever it is, it looks delicious,' said Isabelle, her mouth watering at the sight of the juicy fruit.

The moment she said that, the monkeys started shaking the branches, and the fruit, the size of cherries, started to fall like hail stones to the ground all around them.

'They understood you,' said Holly.

'*Ha*, they did, didn't they?' said Isabelle.

'Yeah, Izzy knows monkey talk,' Jack said, sniggering.

'That's better than stupid talk,' said Akira.

The usual exchange of hot words ensued between these two, more amusing than annoying this time, until they finally stuck their tongues out at each other for good measure.

'Try one, they're delicious,' said Finn.

'Just peel back the furry skin,' Holly told Isabelle.

'I'm trying to, but my nails are too short.'

'Here, let me do it for you,' said Holly.

As Isabelle bit into the soft flesh, saliva filled her mouth and her lips glistened with juice. The smell made her mouth water, but it was the mixture of sweet and sour that made her drool.

'Yum,' said Holly, between mouthfuls.

'Looks weird, but tastes great,' said Jack.

'It's sooo good,' said Isabelle, licking her sticky fingers.

The treetops were soon crowded with monkeys, including several females carrying babies. They looked down on the GeeBees, laughing loudly and chatting noisily together, as if making observations on the tea party going on below them.

Having taken the edge off their rumbling stomachs, Captain M and his little gang set off once more down the path into the undergrowth. The whooping monkeys accompanied them along the canopy above, rushing backwards and forwards, jumping from one tree to the next.

It would be at least another four hours of hiking until the group reached the place where they would camp for the night. So, to pass the time as they walked, Captain M struck up a conversation about the sorts of things that made each one of them happy; what they most enjoyed doing and what sort of hopes and dreams they had for their lives. He asked them all sorts of questions and no matter what he asked, there was always an eager reply.

'And finally, what one thing would you love to do? Something that you believe could also make the world a better place?'

Nobody said anything. They couldn't, because they had never been asked such a question before and weren't quite sure how to answer.

'No one?' the Captain said, laughing. 'I thought that might surprise you.'

Akira, the one person who always had something to say about something, finally spoke.

'You mean, what job do we want to do?'

'Not exactly,' replied the Captain.

His last question was more to do with what would make them feel happy, excited and proud of their achievements. Something they could do that would make a positive mark on the world?'

'Think freely and remember, anything is effiktable if you really, really want it.'

'Well, I want to be able to save people's lives,' said Akira, confidently.

More specifically, she wanted to be a brain surgeon. For Akira, it was much more than cutting people open and sewing them back together again. She imagined herself putting on a surgical mask, scrubbing her hands before surgery, and saving the world.

'Gross! Just think of all that blood,' Jack said.

'Have you got something better to say?' Akira said, sneeringly.

Jack couldn't imagine himself stuck indoors, especially in a cold operating theatre. His dream was to be a photographer.

'Maybe for National Geographic,' he said.

Whenever he went urban exploring with his cousin, his GoPro camera went with him to record the moment.

'We left in such a hurry, I didn't bring it with me,' he said.

For the time being, he would simply have to observe, chronicle, and take imaginary photos with his eyes.

Finn wanted to be a top scientist, an astrophysicist maybe, like his mum. He was always imagining how he could change the way humans travelled through different parts of space and time.

'You mean, like time travel?' Isabelle said.

'Yes, in some kind of time machine,' said Finn.

'*Ohh*, you mean you want to be a watch-maker,' said Jack 'so you can watch time fly!'

He burst out laughing, half collapsing into Finn.

'Nooo,' said Finn, his cheeks turning red.

'*Ha, ha,* very funny Jack,' Akira said, with a straight face.

Finn adjusted his glasses, which had fallen down his nose.

'I ...' he started to say something.

'Or maybe an optician and make x-ray glasses to see into the future,' said Jack, interrupting him once again.

'Shut up Jack,' snapped Akira.

'Jack, please leave him alone,' Isabelle said.

She hated bullies, especially the ones that used the disguise of humour to put down or torment other people.

'Can no one take a joke,' replied Jack, gruffly.

He stomped off ahead, mumbling something about infuriating girls. Then, about five or six feet in front of the others, he stopped dead in his tracks.

'What the ... '

He froze, throwing his arms out, as if he was trying to stop himself from falling forwards, hardly daring to even breathe.

'What's wrong, Jack?' said Holly, from behind.

He shook his head and motioned for everyone to stay where they were. Just inches from his face was a humungous spider, dangling perilously in the middle of an enormous web. Woven between two trees, it stretched like a tennis net across the width of the path.

'Is that what I think it is,' said Isabelle.

'*Wow*, I had no idea they could get that big,' said Finn,

Almost the size of Jack's head, the creature had sinister red markings all over its head, and a hairy black body. It abruptly inflated its abdomen like a puffer fish, and raised its two long forelegs, as if poised to attack if Jack so much as moved an inch.

'Stay completely still.'

The Captain was by Jack's side within seconds. With a long stick in his hand, he started pulling the strands of the web to one side.

'Now, when I say go, pass underneath quickly.'

He spoke so quietly, his voice was almost inaudible. Jack gulped, his eyes fixed on the spider as it stared back at him menacingly, with its multiple eyes. At one moment, he even thought he heard the spider speak to him,

'Beware! My fangs are deadly.'

'Did you hear that?' Jack said, out of the corner of his mouth.

'Hear what?' said Holly.

'I think he's talking about the spider,' said Isabelle in an equally hushed voice.

'Really? A talking spider,' said Akira, tutting.

The web was extremely tough, and the strands creaked, becoming glued to the stick as the Captain carefully pushed them aside.

'One, two three … go,' said the Captain.

Jack crouched low and darted frantically under the web. Once across, he rolled up his sleeves and made a dismissive '*pfff*' sound with his lips, as if it was the easiest thing he had ever done.

'Yeah right,' Akira hissed.

'Quick, all of you pass now,' said the Captain.

One by one, they all crossed under the spidery boobytrap, continuing on their journey as the trail wound up and down, cutting through the jungle.

Holly decided to pick up where Finn had left off in the conversation.

'Well, I don't know what I could do to make a difference.'

She got hold of a twig and swung it left and right, flicking at the vegetation.

'Imagine this is a magic wand,' said Captain M, tapping the twig. 'You can be or do or have anything you want in the world, and remember, if you really want something badly enough, it's effiktable.'

Holly stared at the twig for a few moments, until it dawned on her where she wanted to be in a few years from now.

'Wimbledon tennis tournament,' she said, twirling the branch in the air like a magic wand.

Just the idea of being a top tennis player, and performing on centre court in front of hundreds of people, made her whole face light up.

'That's what I'd love to do. And so many people watch tennis, don't they?' she said.

The Captain nodded and smiled a big yes.

'And what about you, Izzy?'

Isabelle hesitated, looking embarrassed. She found it hard to say what she knew she wanted to say.

'Take the wand,' said Holly.

Isabelle took the twig in her hand, shut her eyes and for a moment thought with all the feelings from her heart. The one thing that always gave her a thrill and she felt good about doing, was being on stage.

'An actress,' she said.

Opening one eye only, Isabelle looked left and right, hoping in a way that no one had paid attention to her. She scanned everyone's reactions, thinking they were secretly laughing at her.

'You kept that one quiet,' said Akira.

'Why not? She was in the Christmas play,' said Holly.

Jack's voice piped up from the front of the group,

'But you've got to be really talented and pretty, haven't you?'

Isabelle cringed, wishing she could take back what she had said.

'Do you think you've got what it takes to learn all those lines?' said Akira.

Akira hadn't meant to be mean, but her comment left Isabelle feeling deflated. A prickly, cold sensation raced around every inch of her body, leaving her wishing she hadn't been so quick to share her dream with everyone.

'Well, I could always become a stagehand instead,' she said, half-heartedly.

Isabelle managed to crack a little smile, just enough to cover any embarrassment she felt.

'It's not the same as acting, but it doesn't really matter,' she thought, trying to console herself. 'Behind the scenes makes more sense.'

Captain M, who was in the background listening to everything that was going on, spoke up.

'So, tell me again, Izzy, what's your dream?'

'To be a stagehand and help behind the scenes in the theatre.'

Isabelle flicked at the undergrowth with the twig, purposefully avoiding the Captain's eyes. Her answer was not so truthful. She knew it and the Captain knew it. He frowned, his bushy eyebrows meeting in the middle, and repeated his question in a slightly different way.

'I mean what do you really, really want to be or do that will make a difference?'

Isabelle stared at him with uncertainty in her eyes, trying to reply in the frankest voice she could muster.

'*Umm … err*,' was all that came out.

'Go on,' the Captain said, giving her a reassuring smile.

'I'd like to be an actress and entertain people, you know, make them happy. But I don't think I can,' she said.

'What makes you believe you can't?' said the Captain.

'There's plenty of other people who'll be better than me,' she answered.

'Wouldn't it be possible, though, if you were willing to put in the hard work and practise as hard as you can?'

'Well …' Isabelle said.

The word effiktable came into her mind and after a short while she said, 'maybe.'

'If you have a clear intention, focus and practise the skills you need, surely you can achieve anything you set your mind to,' said the Captain.

All eyes instantly fell on Isabelle for her answer.

'Well, I guess so,' she said, making a grimace.

The Captain looked down at Isabelle with kindness in his eyes.

'Anything is effiktable Izzy, if you really believe it is.'

Isabelle mouthed the word effiktable quietly to herself.

'And you must be prepared to take one hundred percent responsibility for the outcome of your efforts,' the Captain then added.

'What do you mean?' asked Isabelle.

'Well, being responsible means not making excuses or blaming anyone else if things don't go the way you expect them to go,' the Captain said.

Being asked to accept full responsibility for her actions was a sobering and rather scary thought. Yet it was also exciting. It meant that if Isabelle was the one in control, only she could be held accountable for how much effort she made to accomplish all that she wanted.

'Yep, I think – I mean I believe, I can,' she said.

The Captain put his arm around her shoulders and gave her a side hug.

'You have the power inside of you, Izzy - as you all do - to achieve anything, if truly believe you can.'

He looked up to see where the sun was in the sky, determining the time of day.

'Let's push on.'

The trail continued straight through the ever-thickening undergrowth, until it took a sharp turn to the left. Blocking their path as they turned the bend, was a massive tree, standing like a sentry.

Cut right through the middle of the tree was a hollow opening, the size of a giant door. It was triangular in shape, with a twisting branch running horizontally, like a cross bar through the middle.

'That looks like an A, doesn't it?' said Akira.

'What do you mean?' said Jack.

'The letter A,' Akira said, outlining the letter with her finger.

'Oh, yes, so it does,' said Holly.

'Well spotted Akira,' said the Captain. 'A letter which is much more than the first letter of the alphabet.'

'Come again?' said Jack.

The letter A, the Captain explained to them, marked the beginning of all things and expressed the transition from potential to actualization. A transition that the GeeBees themselves would undergo on Aydagar as they discovered the nine Life Secrets.

'Look out for the names of places as we journey through the island,' he told them.

'Like A for Aydagar,' said Finn.

'Yessss,' said Holly.

'That's such a coincidence?' said Isabelle.

The Captain smiled and replied,

'*Ahhh*, but there is no such thing as coincidence, nothing happens by chance.'

He then moved in the direction of a tree stump by the side of the path. It was curved in the middle and made the most perfect chair. Taking off the goatskin water bag that was slung across his shoulders, Captain M sat down, pulling out the leather stop. From his side pocket, he removed six small metal cups, which he filled with water and passed around to everyone.

The Captain closed his eyes and made the strange motion with his hands, moving his right fist in a quick anti-clockwise motion over his left palm. He opened one eye, then closed it again, muttering something no-one could understand clearly.

'Every day, we all have different types of thoughts,' he said, opening his eyes wide again. 'Some thoughts are fleeting, which means they come and then just go.'

'So, they go in one ear and out the other,' Jack said laughing.

The Captain nodded and smiled.

'They are of no importance and so, like dust in the wind, simply disappear and you give them no more thought.'

'Like most of the thoughts that go through your head Akira,' said Jack.

Akira blew a raspberry at him and he let out a huge, watery burb.

'*Urrr* - you're so disgusting,' said Akira.

'I try my best,' Jack said, putting on his best smile.

Captain M turned to Jack and frowned.

'Let me know when you're ready to listen.'

Jack went quiet and nodded his head back and forth in a manner that was neither a yes nor a no.

'On the other hand,' the Captain continued, 'other thoughts that we have, are more meaningful. I'm talking about the sort of thoughts that have strong feelings attached to them.'

'For example?' said Akira.

'Well, try this. Think back to your birthday,' he said.

Holly's face lit up, and she broke out in a huge smile as she thought back to how grown up and special, she felt on her twelfth birthday. Her parents arranged a party, and friends came to the house to celebrate with her. As if it was yesterday, she remembered all the games they played and how she had so much fun.

'You see, just thinking happy thoughts gives you happy feelings,' said the Captain.

'That's so true,' said Holly.

Isabelle, on the other hand, had a look of quiet sadness as she thought back to her lonely, twelfth birthday.

'They're not always nice feelings that come from our thoughts,' said the Captain. 'Isn't that right, Izzy?'

Isabelle looked at him and hung her head low, shaking it slowly.

'You see, when you think sad thoughts, you then actually begin to feel sad,' he said, looking at them all.

'Just thinking about how I felt, really does make me feel sad all over again,' Isabelle said.

'You see, the thoughts that we think have a very powerful effect on how we feel.'

The Captain shifted in his seat, from side to side, and then leaned forward, as if he was going to say something important. Everyone automatically leaned slightly in, gazing at him in anticipation.

'Some of these thoughts with strong feelings often stick around, coming back again and again and again,' he said.

'*Ohhh,*' said Isabelle, on the verge of saying something, but choosing at the last minute to hold back.

The Captain knew what she wanted to say and encouraged her to give voice to it by saying a long 'yesss Izzy.' His bright green eyes sparkled as he lifted his dark eyebrows to look at her.

'I always believe that I can't do things,' she said.

'And what normally happens?'

'*Umm* … I usually can't do them.'

The Captain nodded his head in agreement.

'Well Izzy, when you think you can't do something, then the likelihood is you won't be able to do it.'

'So, that means that if you think you can, then you probably will be able to,' said Holly.

'That's right,' said the Captain. 'Now listen up closer.'

Leaning further forward, he launched into an explanation of how when thoughts are repeated over and over, they become beliefs.

'A belief is a thought that you have again and again, and one that you no longer question,' he added. 'You just believe it to be true. And Izzy here, has created a belief that she can't do certain things. Now, what you all have to realise is, that your beliefs can either help you achieve what you want, or they can stop you from getting it,' continued the Captain.

'So, the more I think I'm not good enough, then that means I'll always feel that way?' said Isabelle. 'Can't I make those feelings go away?'

'Well, that's the great news, Izzy. You certainly can,' he answered, brightly. 'By changing the way you think.'

The secret, he explained, was to focus hard on what she could do rather than on what she couldn't do; to focus on what she wanted and not on what she didn't want. And in this way, she would start to create new beliefs based around all the things that she wanted and could achieve.

'Keep on focussing on all that you want to be, or do or have,' the Captain said.

Isabelle thought about it for a while, and the more she thought about it, the more it sounded too good to be true.

'So, you mean, I just have to keep on saying to myself that I can do it – and I'll be able to do it?'

The Captain laughed.

'It'll only work if you really, truly believe you can, from deep down inside,' he said, tapping his heart. 'If you think you can, then you'll start feeling that you can, and then most likely you will find that you can.'

'So, let me get this right,' said Akira. 'What you're saying is that we have to create new habits in the way we think.'

'Exactly, Akira,' said the Captain.

'What, just like that?' Holly asked, clicking her thumb and middle finger together.

'No, you can't do it at once,' said the Captain, laughing. 'But if you do something again and again, for some time, without taking a break, then you've clinched it and it becomes a new habit.'

Isabelle examined her badly bitten nails, rough at the ends and sunk into the flesh of her fingers. Then she looked at Holly's beautiful fingertips. Her nails were strong, pink and healthy.

'Can I stop biting my nails,' she asked the Captain.

'Yes Izzy, if you keep on focussing on what you want and not on what you don't want.'

'I want nice, long, nails,' said Isabelle.

'If you're willing to work on the changes you want, then it will surely be effiktable.'

'That's what I want,' Isabelle said.

'Is that the second Life Secret?' asked Holly.

'It is indeed,' said the Captain.

He pulled out his pouch, retrieved a token with the words 'Heart Thoughts' written in the centre on one side and an image of a heart on the other. Running around the perimeter of the token were the same words in Hellenic, 'Skepseis Kardias'.

'This is for you, bubbly Holly,' the Captain said, handing her the token.

'It's a heart,' she said.

The Captain nodded and stood up, stretching as he straightened.

'Remember, the feelings that you feel from your heart are closely linked to the thoughts that you think in your mind.'

'Think happy thoughts and you feel good,' said Holly.

'Think unhappy thoughts, and you feel bad,' said Isabelle.

'Bravo!' said the Captain, clapping his hands together.

He then made his way towards the curiously shaped hollow in the trunk where Jack was already standing.

'This tree must be hundreds of years old,' said Jack, throwing stones into the hollow.

Strangely, the heartwood was gone and yet the tree's vast, strong branches were as alive as the younger trees that surrounded it.

The Captain gestured for Jack to pass through.

'It smells old and woody,' said Jack, ducking while passing through.

'This'd be a great place to sleep,' said Finn.

'Too damp for me,' Akira said, crossing through.

'I think it's kind of cosy,' said Holly.

Before walking through, Isabelle gave one last look at the Captain and smiled.

'If I think I can, then I'll prove myself right,' she said.

She watched the Captain's smiley face as if she knew exactly what he was going to say next.

'When you know what you want and want it badly enough, then, without a doubt, it becomes effiktable.'

5

SINEFIASMENOS KATHREFTIS
*
SMOKY MIRROR

Like a train of ants, the explorers briskly followed their guide along an ever-narrowing dirt trail until eventually they came out to the sea again. This time to a pebbled beach that opened up a full view of the remainder of the Power Coast.

A strong sea breeze blew in from the sea, touching their faces and whispering supernatural sounds, their meaning beyond comprehension. The fragrance of the salty air mingled strangely with the sweet fragrance of white flowers dotted all around the beach.

Overhead, seagulls hovered in the air, swooping down and then curving up again.

'*Kaa kaa,*' they vented a series of loud squawking cries.

The GeeBee's first day on the island was slowly coming to its end. The colours of the horizon were gradually changing from a fine violet blue tint to spectacular shades of orange and red.

Bit by bit the group made their way along the beach to a makeshift shelter. Its roof was slanted like a tent, covered with palm leaves and split bamboo. Lying on the soft straw flooring were six mats with sheets made of large banana leaves.

'This is our resting place for the night,' said the Captain.

'I can't go to sleep here,' said Akira.

She prodded one of the makeshift beds, which gave off a groaning sound.

'What was that?' she said.

'*Wow*, even the beds talk here,' said Holly.

'If you choose to sleep or not, it's up to you. But this is where we're camping for the night,' the Captain answered earnestly, looking into Akira's eyes.

'I'm starving,' said Jack.

'Me too, me too,' they all agreed.

'Well then, help yourselves to something to eat.'

The Captain pointed towards a large woven basket under a nearby tree, packed with an assortment of tropical fruit, alongside bread rolls, pancakes and pastries.

'Goody, I'm famished,' said Finn.

'Not as hungry as me,' said Jack, pushing his way past Finn to open the basket.

The GeeBees lost no time in asking permission to eat their supper as they had to do at school, and tucked into their meal. Everyone ate and ate until they were too full to eat any more.

'I'm stuffed,' said Holly, flopping back against a tree.

'I've had an ample sufficiency.'

Only Akira could say something like that. She had this knack of rendering even the simplest of thoughts into a sentence that was quite convoluted.

'Who talks like that?' said Jack. 'Do you have to sound so

posh all the time? It's so stupid.'

'Stupid for someone simple-minded like you,' said Akira.

But before the two could start off again on one of their usual tit-for-tat showdowns, the Captain removed the leather water container from his back, and held it in the air.

'Izzy, would you mind coming with me to get some fresh water?'

'Sure,' she responded, still munching on her apple.

'What are we going to do?' said Finn.

'Spend some time on the beach,' said the Captain. 'It's low tide, so you can even reach the rock pools over there. But don't fall in the water.'

'Yeess!' they all said triumphantly, and walked down to the water's edge.

Finn picked up a handful of round, flat pebbles and started skimming them on the water's surface. Jack rolled up his trouser legs and waded into the shallow waters, lured by the red-orange star fish and spiky sea urchins clinging tightly to the rocks nearby.

Holly and Akira aimed for the rocks where an assortment of tiny, darting fish were trapped in the warm, shallow pools of water left by the receding waves.

'They're almost see-through,' said Akira.

'*Haaa*, look at their bones,' said Holly.

As the girls examined the miniature marine life, the Captain and Isabelle began their walk inland. Taking a different path to the one they were previously on, they walked for a few hundred feet until they reached a small lake.

The water was like glass and it reflected the clouds and sky like a mirror. Isabelle dropped to her knees in the soft grass around the lake's edge, mesmerized by the clouds as they seemingly moved over the surface of the water.

Cupping her cheeks in her hands, she leaned over and noticed her own reflection in the liquid mirror. As she looked at herself, the water became slightly clouded, as if a veil of smoke was blowing lightly just over the surface.

She stared hard, squinting at herself, struggling to bring her reflection into focus. But her eyes could only make out the blemishes and imperfections in her appearance.

She gave out a big, loud sigh.

'Tell me, what do you see?' asked Captain M.

Isabelle gave an automatic response without looking up at her guide.

'Oh, nothing special, just me,' she answered, with a quiet sadness.

'Nothing or something?' the Captain insisted.

Isabelle glanced up at him with a questioning look on her face, then back down at the water. As she stared at her reflection, she wondered what it was that other people saw in her.

'My left eye's lower than the right one and they're definitely both a different shape.'

Isabelle turned her head half-heartedly to the left and right, as she continued to study her face.

'And look at my nose - it's huge.'

Worse still, the little fiery spots sprinkled over her cheeks made her feel like she wanted to hide. There were no ifs and buts about it; Isabelle thought she was as plain as plain could be. Not a single ounce of prettiness in her.

Suddenly feeling uncomfortable, she looked up at the Captain and smiled. But the smile didn't feel quite real. It was more like one of those fake smiles that you see painted around the mouth of a circus clown.

'Even my smile is crooked,' she mumbled.

'Anything else?' said the Captain.

'Well, my neck's long and bony. I look just like a giraffe,' she said, lifting her chin.

As Isabelle became lost in her world of negative thoughts, Captain M picked up a small stone and tossed it into the water just in front of her. This sent ripples outwards in circles, completely distorting the image of her face.

He then sat down next to her and fumbled in his breast pocket, taking out two gold coins. One coin was bright and looked brand new, whilst the other was misshapen, dirty and had lost its shine.

'Are they the tokens?' she asked him.

'No,' the Captain answered. 'Just two gold coins.'

He turned them over in his hand, studying them closely until his expression changed.

'I think I'll get rid of this one,' he said.

He raised his arm upwards and started to make a throwing motion through the air.

'No, don't,' Isabelle shouted out.

'Why not? It doesn't look like it's worth much.'

'But, but …' she said stumbling over her words. 'It must still be worth a lot.'

Captain M smiled warmly at her and said,

'*Ahhh*, really?'

The next thought was clearly echoing in his mind as he placed both coins on the open palm of his right hand.

'So, in your mind, this tarnished coin has the same value as this shiny one?'

'Of course,' Isabelle replied.

'So, what you're saying Izzy is, even if something isn't

perfect on the outside, that doesn't mean it holds less value than something that seems outwardly perfect?'

Isabelle stared deep into the Captain's striking eyes, quickly understanding where he was going with this.

'But I don't say bad things about myself out loud,' she said.

'Izzy, it's not just what you say out loud that counts,' he told her. 'It's also all the things you whisper silently to yourself in your head.'

The Captain settled himself more comfortably and crossed his legs as he continued his explanation.

'You see Izzy, the thoughts and words that you think and say to yourself every day, are even more powerful than the thoughts that you put into words and say out loud.'

'Am I the only one that does that?'

'Of course not. Everyone does it.'

'But I don't actually talk to myself,' Isabelle said, pulling a funny face.

'Oh, yes you do. We all do, much of the time,' Captain M said in an emphatic voice.

He then went on to tell her that the thoughts that she thought and the words that she said to herself every day were called *self-talk*.

'But only crazy people talk to themselves.'

Isabelle giggled, thinking she was being funny.

'There's nothing wrong with people talking to themselves,' continued the Captain, 'but I'm talking to you about the type of self-talk that can cause you harm. This is something that most people don't know about.'

'What, not even grown-ups?' said Isabelle.

'Not even,' said the Captain.

'I still - don't really understand.'

'Self-talk, Izzy, is the way that we communicate with ourselves. It's a voice inside our heads that can help cheer us on and make us feel great, both about ourselves and the world around us. Or it can also be a negative, self-defeating voice that makes us feel quite unhappy.'

He reminded her of the second Life Secret, about how closely linked thoughts and feelings were to each other.

'Heart thoughts,' she said quietly.

'That's right.'

Isabelle immediately remembered how nice, positive thoughts filled her with hope; whereas negative thoughts, filled her with a strong feeling of sadness.

'If I said to you, "you're a failure". How does that make you feel?' the Captain asked her.

The answer to this was obvious in Isabelle's mind, and she answered without hesitation.

'Not very nice.'

Changing his tone of voice, the Captain asked her another question.

'How about if I tell you, "you're amazing"?'

Isabelle lifted her head on hearing that word, and her face instantly lit up, like the sun in the sky. In fact, her whole-body posture changed. She sat up straight, seemingly taller than she was before.

'Nice, really nice.'

'Well, look at that,' said the Captain. 'That positive word had the power to make you sit upright and strong.'

Moving from a sad to a happy feeling, Isabelle had even thrown her shoulders back without realising. She wasn't slouching, as her mother always complained that she was.

'Now, the problem is, most people are prone to negative

self-talk, rather than positive self-talk.'

Captain M bent down and slurped some water from the lake, swishing it in his mouth. As he did so, he gave Isabelle a knowing look out of the corner of his eye, before swallowing with a big gulp.

'Like - when I think I'm not good enough?' said Isabelle.

Together with these thoughts came others that she had often said to herself in the past; thoughts like 'I'm so stupid' and 'I'm such a failure.' Just playing those words in her mind, made Isabelle shake her head and lower her eyes once again.

'As I said before, Izzy, you may not be saying the words out loud, but just thinking them can have an even stronger impact on you,' said the Captain.

Until this moment, Isabelle hadn't realised just how many negative thoughts she had swirling in her head about herself. And when she understood this, she also made the decision that she preferred to have happier thoughts and feel happier feelings about herself.

'So, how can I stop it all?' she said.

There was a mixture of captivation and uncertainty on Isabelle's face as she gazed at the Captain, waiting for a solution.

'You just *shift your focus*,' he told her.

'What does that mean?'

'Change the way you think about yourself,' he said in a very matter-of-fact way. 'Believe it or not, it's up to you to decide what you want to focus on; good or bad, negative or positive.'

'But that's so difficult,' said Isabelle.

'It's only seems difficult because you've got used to doing things a certain way,' answered the Captain.

She looked at her bitten nails, remembering their earlier conversation about breaking an old habit and creating a new one.

'Negative self-talk is just a bad habit, that makes you think and feel badly about yourself so much of the time,' he said.

'Can I really decide how I talk to myself?' Isabelle asked.

'Of course, you can - by shifting your focus and turning your thinking around.'

'You mean, from negative to positive?' asked Isabelle.

The Captain nodded.

'What could I say instead of, I can't?' said Isabelle.

'Think about it for a moment, Izzy, you have all the answers inside of you.'

Isabelle shrugged her shoulders automatically and bit her bottom lip, as she often did, not really sure how to answer the question. But she took a guess anyway.

'I can always try hard and do my best,' she said.

'What a great answer,' said the Captain.

Hope welled up inside Isabelle as she wondered about how great it would be if she could change around how she thought about herself.

'But you've got to really, really believe what you say,' said the Captain. 'And really feel it, as if it's true and as if it's already happened.'

Isabelle looked down again into the water with a new sense of determination. As she did so, she noticed that her reflection was now somehow different. It was as if she was looking at herself for the first time.

'You are so much greater than you think you are Izzy,' said the Captain.

'That's what Whisper said to me.'

Tinkle - tinkle - ting-a-ling.

Isabelle smiled on hearing Whisper, and as she looked down

again at the water, she noticed that it was no longer smoky, but clear. Her face broke into such a genuine broad smile.

Everything became strangely silent as her gaze slipped downwards towards her neck. She swept her brown, shoulder-length hair up at the back with one hand, and stared at a long, elegant swan-like neck.

As her eyes wandered down a little further, she saw the most extraordinary thing. On either side behind her shoulders, were two little feathery tufts. Isabelle's eyes shot wide open, then blinked in surprise.

'What's that?'

Her reflection started to change right before her very eyes. Wings started sprouting from the back of her shoulders, but when she turned her head to take a look there was nothing there. She placed her right hand across her left shoulder but could feel nothing.

Isabelle looked back at her reflection, only it wasn't her anymore. It was a cherub-like face of a boy, with lovely white skin. Isabelle sat up straight with a jolt, looking at the Captain and then straight back at her new reflection.

'Who's that?' she whispered, scared that she might frighten the winged being.

'Izzy,' the Captain replied in a hushed voice. 'Meet your guardian angel.'

As if he had been waiting for this introduction, the angel began gently flapping his wings. Slowly lifting out of the water, he now became lifelike as he hovered on the surface in front of her.

'Hello Izzy. I'm Aziel, your angel guide,' he said.

'He knows my name?' said Isabelle.

'Like Whisper, he knows everything about you Izzy,' replied

the Captain.

A soft purple glow began to surround Aziel, like an aura. As Isabelle stared in disbelief, the light slowly became brighter and began to pulsate like a heartbeat. This made no sense to Isabelle at all, yet she felt the same deep sense of comfort and safety that she felt when she first met Whisper.

Tinkle - tinkle - ting-a-ling.

Isabelle smiled once more, feeling Whisper inside her, beside her and all around her.

'I watch over you Izzy and help keep you out of harm's way,' said Aziel, in a dreamy voice.

'Mmm … me?' said Isabelle.

She silently watched her glowing angel as he turned around and slowly started drifting across the lake. His toes dangled in the crystal-clear water, leaving ripples behind him. As he floated towards the centre of the lake, the Captain took the time to explain some things about angels.

'Angels are spiritual beings of love and light that work to help us in our lifetime,' he told her.

'He said he was my angel,' said Isabelle.

'Just like everyone has a secret voice inside them called Whisper, so do we all have our very own guardian angel.'

Isabelle sat still, half listening and half dumbfounded. She certainly had not expected her time on Aydagar to be so full of surprises.

'Aziel will always respect your free will and will never directly interfere in your life, unless you ask him to,' continued the Captain.

Aziel stopped in the middle of the lake and without warning, started spinning like a top. The faster his movements became, the brighter his light shone; until suddenly, and for no apparent reason, the wild spinning stopped.

The angelic figure turned towards Isabelle, looked her straight in the eyes and softly said,

'Remember I am always in and around you
And with my love I will always surround you
When in your heart you feel a slight tug
Just call my name for an angel hug.'

And with that, Aziel laughed out loud and disappeared into a cloud of sparkling, purple-blue smoke.

Isabelle sat spell-bound on the grassy bank. She gazed into the middle of the lake, her head full of a thousand thoughts.

'Remember your angel is ever around you,' she hummed his last words.

The next voice she heard was the Captain's.

'Using positive self-talk, Izzy, will also help you draw your angel closer to you.'

The Captain looked up at the pinkie-grey sky through the trees, and silently thanked Aziel for appearing to Isabelle. He took a few long breaths, savouring the moment.

'We should be getting back to the others now.'

The Captain filled his container until the water reached the top and spilled over a little.

'*Whoa*, that was sooo awesome,' said Isabelle.

As she replayed every precious moment that had just taken place in her mind, the Captain was looking through his pouch. He removed the third secret token and gave it to Isabelle. She read both sets of engraved words out loud.

'Smoky Mirror … Sin-efias-menos Kath-reftis.'

The Captain nodded and smiled.

'Just as the water has the power to shift and mould the earth's landscape, your thoughts have the power to shift and mould your life as well.'

Not every twelve-year-old girl got the chance to meet her guardian angel, that was for sure. And as far as Isabelle was concerned, she would do everything in her power to keep her thoughts positive, in the hope that she would once again meet Aziel.

She ran back down the path towards her friends who had been waiting, waving and smiling. Without a moment's pause, she started to explain in great detail all that had taken place.

'You mean we all have a guardian angel?' asked Akira.

'Yes, every single one of us has,' Isabelle said.

'So, we've got a Whisper and a guardian angel,' gasped Holly.

'*Wow*, that's pretty awesome,' said Finn.

'Isn't it just?' said Isabelle, clapping her hands.

'You know, Izzy - I don't know exactly, but there's something different about you,' said Jack.

He thought for a minute.

'You seem taller or something,' he added.

Akira could also see that Isabelle was somehow different. Was it the way her friend spoke or stood? She wasn't sure either. All she knew, was that everything Isabelle said was full of colour and light.

'You're all sparkly,' Holly said, giving her friend a squeezy hug.

Learning about positive and negative self-talk and seeing that she was just as special as the next person, had indeed made Isabelle shine from head to toe.

The sun by now had set and the explorers were exhausted. There was no getting away from that. They were all quite happy to just collapse into bed and go to sleep.

'*Ahhh*,' said Akira, sighing with relief as she took off

her shoes.

She lay down happily on her mattress.

'It's quite comfy,' said Holly, as she pulled the banana leaf over her body.

'Good night everyone, sweet dreams,' said the Captain.

The GeeBees all said their goodnights and soon they drifted away into a sea of sleep.

Only Isabelle remained half awake, mesmerised by the ocean of glittering stars sprinkled across the night sky. She was starting to believe, not only in the magic of wishes, but in herself, too.

At that very moment she saw a star wink at her and then shoot across the sky. And so, she made a wish.

'I wish …' she whispered sleepily.

Then she made another wish, and then another, until she, too, fell asleep dreaming of all the possibilities that her life might bring.

MONSTER CAVES

6

VALE ORIA
*
DRAW THE LINE

The whole island started to wake up early the next morning, just before dawn. Palm leaves rustled in the light sea breeze, while the waves unceasingly came and went, licking the pebbled shoreline. The delicate sound of a single bird chirping soon amplified, as a multitude of birds joined in, whistling their early morning song.

Still heavy with sleep, Isabelle slowly woke up to these sounds, rubbing the shadows of sleep from her eyes. Hazy images of her dreams played in her mind but as she tried to recapture them, she found she couldn't. The dreams were gone.

'Hello you,' said Akira.

'*Ohh*, hiya,' said Isabelle.

'Good morning to you,' the Captain said, cheerily. 'Anyone for breakfast?'

'I'll have - two - cheeseburgers,' said Finn, yawning in-between each word.

'And chips,' came Holly's chirpy voice.

They both burst into laughter as they sat up. Jack groaned loudly, covered his head with the palm leaf and rolled over.

'Go on then, tuck in,' said the Captain.

He pointed towards the same woven basket from the day before, only now it was now packed with a new supply of food.

'Finn, make me a sandwich,' Jack ordered his friend.

'You've got two hands, make it yourself,' said Akira.

She grinned at Finn who smiled back at her in appreciation.

'*Uggh*, terrible service,' said Jack.

He dragged himself out of bed and joined the others, who were already bolting down their breakfast.

It was not long before the sun crept up over the eastern horizon, flooding the sea and sky with a host of colours - yellows, oranges, pinks and reds - one after the other.

'Is everyone ready to move on?' asked Captain M.

'Just a mo,' said Jack, stuffing the last of the bread rolls into his pocket.

'We're ready,' said Akira, as usual speaking on everyone's behalf.

Within minutes, the explorers were walking away from the camp site, clambering over an outcrop of rocks and making their way along the beach. At the far end, the stretch of shoreline ended abruptly with a sheer rock face that reached at least seventy feet in height.

A flight of roughly cut stone steps led upwards like a staircase, moving up the face of the cliff to the top. Each step was uneven but smooth, and looked as if it had been climbed upon by thousands of feet.

'Were these made for giants?' said Finn, standing at the foot of the deep, wide steps.

'They were actually made by the Andriots,' said Captain M.

'You mean, there's other people here apart from us?' said Akira.

Although the island was full of animal life, so far there had been no signs of human life anywhere. Finn asked the question that was on everybody's mind.

'Who are they?'

'The Andriots were an exceptionally tall race of people who lived here at one time,' said the Captain.

Many different indigenous groups had made Aydagar their home, but the Andriots were the oldest.

'Are we going to get to meet them?' said Holly, excitedly.

'How can we meet them?' Akira snapped at Holly. 'Didn't you hear him? He said, *at one time* - which means they're no longer here.'

'Oh, I didn't think,' said Holly.

'Just follow me and you'll find out their fate,' said Captain M.

By now, everyone had noticed that the Captain often avoided giving them a straight answer to their questions. It was almost as if he sometimes wanted to keep them on tenterhooks.

He began to climb the giant, weatherworn steps that had been carved so many centuries ago into the rock. The ascent looked extremely steep and almost impossible from the bottom.

'Come on,' said Isabelle, beginning the climb.

'I'll never make it up there' said Akira.

'Just put one foot in front of the other,' said Jack, pushing deliberately past her.

'Get off me,' reacted Akira.

'Just stick close to me.'

Holly slipped her hand into Akira's, as they began the climb together, side by side. The higher they got, the more nervous

Akira became and the more her hand stuck to Holly's. No one spoke very much, carefully focussing on where they placed their feet. Patches of sand and loose stones littered the steps, making it easy to slip and fall at any moment.

'Are we nearly there?' said Akira, huffing and panting.

She dared not look up in case she lost her footing and dared not look down for fear of dizziness, so she kept her eyes fixed on the step in front of her.

'Come on Akira,' said Holly tugging at her hand, 'this is meant to be fun.'

'Yeah, as much fun as chewing on razor blades.'

Akira stopped short of the last three steps, huffing and panting heavily. Starting to feel shaky, she wasn't sure if she'd make it to the top.

'Just a bit more,' Isabelle called from the top.

Holly gave Akira a few final yanks up the last steps until finally, they had all reached the summit of the cliff. Turning around full circle from where they were standing, they could see everything around for miles: a kaleidoscope of beautiful greyish-pinks, bluey-purples, and cotton wool whites all mixed together.

It was warmer up here and the only sound to be heard, was the constant background breeze rustling through the long grass, and the occasional crickets chirping their hypnotic song.

'Did you know that crickets make that noise by rubbing their wings together,' said Finn.

'Really?' said Isabelle.

But before he had the chance to continue his explanation, Jack butted in.

'And that's interesting because …?'

Finn felt hot; prickly bumps climbed up his neck as he tried to answer Jack back, but he just couldn't. He just swallowed his jumbled words.

'Well, I for one didn't know that,' said Akira.

'And why am I not surprised about that,' said Jack.

'Do you always have to be so horrible?' Isabelle said.

'What's your problem?' said Jack, turning his nastiness onto Isabelle.

'Come on everyone, onwards we go,' Captain M interrupted, loudly.

Once more the explorers were on the move, heading down a dusty path that ran along the cliff, and then northwards. The surroundings here were wild and rugged, a stark contrast to the tropical jungle they had just left behind.

The GeeBees followed the Captain like mountain goats, carefully manoeuvring their way through a rocky terrain of prickly bushes, peculiar flowering cacti, and delicate shrubs. Wild oregano and thyme crunched under their feet and sent up a powerfully aromatic scent.

'Keep away from the edges,' said the Captain, stamping his feet hard with every step he took.

He warned them that the deep pockets of leaves either side of the trail were a great hiding place for the sinister Fidi, a species of tri-tongued snake commonly found in this part of the island.

'Are they poisonous?' Finn asked the Captain.

'No, but their bite's pretty painful,' the Captain replied. 'So, watch out.'

'*Whoa*, look over there,' gasped Isabelle.

Both she and Holly started to run headlong, towards what looked like the ruins of an old settlement. Comprised of only a series of stone slabs sitting squarely on each other, with just the chimney and fireplace still intact, these crumbled cottages dotted the whole hill side.

'Did people really live here once?' asked Jack.

'Yes. These were once the homes of the Andriots,' answered the Captain.

'So where did everyone go?' said Akira.

'No one knows for sure,' said the Captain, 'but it's said that in the time of my ancestors, a great force of nature completely destroyed this beautiful place.'

'What force?' said Finn.

'What happened?' asked Holly.

'A terrible dark monster called Sizmos - the earth shaker - lay in hibernation beneath the village. With seven fearful dragon heads that flashed fire and made unspeakable screeches of fury, Sizmos woke up one day and managed to break through the earth's crust to the surface.'

The Captain's eyes gleamed with anguish, and his whole face moved as he told the story, every muscle working extra hard in describing the chaos and destruction that took place. At one point, Akira's eyes strained so much that they looked as if they would pop out of her head.

'When Sizmos tried to take supremacy of the whole of Aydagar, all the tribes of the island joined forces with the elves, sprites and magical forest creatures in order to defeat the beast.'

'Did they get it?' Jack said.

The Captain simply shook his head in dismay.

'Noooo,' said Holly, exhaling noisily.

'Where did the monster go?' asked Isabelle, gripped.

'Yeah, what happened?' asked Jack.

'Most people say that Sizmos fled once again into darkness.'

'Back, under the earth?' said Akira.

'To the darkness of the caves over there,' the Captain answered, pointing in the direction they were heading.

'You mean, the Monster Caves?' asked Holly.

The Captain gave another simple nod of his head.

'But that's where we're going,' said Finn.

'You're kidding, right?' said Jack.

Jack considered himself brave, but not brave enough to take on a fire-breathing monster in the dark.

Captain M smiled and gave a little chuckle that was so characteristic of him.

'It's just one of the legends that the people of Aydagar made up, trying to make sense of what they didn't understand about the world.'

'Like what?' said Finn.

'Earthquakes and other inexplicable forces of nature,' said Captain M.

'Legend or no legend, you won't catch me going into those caves,' said Jack, adamantly.

'Me neither,' added Akira.

'Finally, they agree on something!' said Holly.

'The caves you fear to enter hold two important Life Secrets that you seek,' said the Captain.

He tilted his head to one side and gave them an all-knowing look, as if to say, 'you don't have much choice in the matter.'

'You'll be with us, right?' Holly asked him.

'Close by, as always.'

The group made their way through this no man's land, to the very top of the hill until they reached a bamboo grove on a sort of plateau. Pushing their way through the reeds for a short while, they came out to a rope bridge that stretched across a raging river hundreds of feet below.

'You cannot be serious?' said Akira, her eyes glued to the rickety bridge. 'We're really going to cross that?'

'This is awesome,' said Finn.

'Totally,' said Holly, rubbing her hands in excitement.

Made of wooden planks tied together by old ropes, the bridge seemed quite slack and sagged in the middle.

'It looks like it could snap under us,' said Akira.

'Will it take our weight?' Finn asked the Captain.

'Well, it always has - so far,' answered the Captain.

'Was he joking? He has to be joking,' said Akira.

'Of course, he is! You're kidding, right, Captain M?' said Isabelle.

The Captain winked and gave them his perfect smile.

'Now, down to business,' he continued. 'Hold onto the sides the whole time while you're crossing.'

He pointed to the two rope handrails on either side of the bridge.

'Face forwards and most importantly, no looking down. You all got that?'

There was a mixture of excited nodding and bewildered shaking of heads.

'There's no turning back now,' said the Captain.

He stepped onto the bridge, cautiously testing the first plank with his left foot. It creaked a little but was sturdy, so he continued to move ten more steps forward, and then turned around.

'Who wants to go first?' he called out.

'Me,' said Holly, without a moment's hesitation.

Always light on her feet, Holly started the crossing without even blinking an eye, not even once.

'I'll be right behind the girls,' the Captain told the boys. 'Jack, you're the oldest, so you follow Finn.'

'Come on then, we're next,' Isabelle told Akira.

Carefully positioning their feet while holding tightly onto the handrail, they both began the crossing. Once the girls and Captain M were halfway across, Jack turned around to Finn and said,

'Our turn.'

'I'll go in front,' said Finn.

'No, I'll go,' said Jack.

'But the Captain …' Finn started saying.

'But the Captain,' Jack repeated his words mockingly.

He gave a scornful laugh and jumped onto the bridge with a massive thud.

'This'll be fun,' he thought, grinning devilishly.

Finn started the crossing after Jack, shunting forwards slowly with no idea what awaited him. Without warning, Jack stopped in his tracks and slowly turned his head around. His face creased up and his eyes glinted mischievously. Then he let go of the railings and spun around, so he was now facing Finn.

'What are you doing?' cried out Finn.

Jack glared at him and started to swing his body from left to right, bobbing up and down as if the bridge was a trampoline. Finn looked ahead to the Captain, but he was engrossed in a conversation with the girls.

Although he knew he wasn't supposed to, Finn couldn't help himself and looked down. Through the spaces in between the planks, he could see the gushing water below and for a few moments, thought he would poop his pants.

'I dare you to let go,' Jack, threatened.

Finn's whole body froze. Even his lips felt numb. His heart started pumping wildly and when he tried to open his mouth to speak, he just couldn't put the words together.

'Run back,' said a voice inside his head, but his body wouldn't let him.

'Let go,' Jack growled.

With no reaction from Finn, Jack held onto the railings even tighter and shook the bridge once again, using the force of his whole body.

Scared to let go but even more scared to hold on, Finn tried to loosen his grip on the railings.

'I can't,' he said frantically.

'You're such a wimp,' said Jack, mocking him once again.

This wasn't the first time that Finn had felt threatened or pressured by his classmate. Jack had often called him names; putting him down for his nerdy love of astronomy, for always raising his hand in class or because of the way he ate. Finn would often wake up in the morning, wondering what Jack would do or say that day that would make him feel like a door mat.

Yet instead of avoiding Jack, Finn reacted to Jack's arm-twisting tactics by remaining silent. If he did speak out, it could possibly mean losing the only friend he had made so far at school. So, Finn learnt to suffer in silence, unable to communicate the distress or resentment that was brewing up inside him.

'I told you to let go,' Jack insisted.

'No,' said a muffled voice from inside Finn's head.

'Go on, do it,' came Jack's loud voice once again.

Everything was becoming a big blur, so much so that Finn felt that he was wearing earplugs. Jack's voice strangely started to move into the background, his words becoming muffled and scarcely intelligible.

Meanwhile, the 'no' voice from inside Finn's head started to become louder and stronger. Until quite out of the blue, the words exploded out of Finn's mouth, like water bursting through a broken damn.

'Cut it out, Jack!' he shouted.

But even his outburst didn't stop Jack from continuing his bullying tactics.

'Make me,' he retorted.

'No,' said Finn. 'Just get out of the way.'

Even though his voice was trembling, there was something different in the way Finn spoke this time; a firmness that showed Jack that he meant business.

So, for the moment Jack backed off.

'You're such a loser,' Jack said, nastily.

But he still wasn't ready to give up without one last fight, willing to risk anything to get what he wanted. As he turned, he jumped on the bridge hard with both feet once again. But this time, the sudden jerk caused one of the old planks to give way beneath him and his right foot ended up slipping through the crack.

'*Aggghhh*, help!' he shrieked, as he straddled the bridge.

Finn grabbed Jack's wrist, but he knew he wasn't strong enough to stop Jack falling if the whole plank gave way. Sheer panic kept both boys hanging tightly onto the railings, until a voice from further down the bridge echoed,

'Hang on.'

Within seconds, Jack felt the Captain's strong hands grabbing him and pulling him up to safety.

'Don't let go,' whimpered Jack.

Clinging onto the Captain, he broke down into sobs.

'You're okay, you're going to be fine,' said the Captain,

tapping him on the shoulder.

'*Phew*, that was close,' said Finn.

'Come on, let's get moving - focus straight ahead,' said the Captain.

The three of them crossed the bridge to the other side, where Jack fell to his knees.

'*Ouch*,' he said, looking at his bleeding leg.

The boys sat in awkward silence for a while, until the Captain spoke.

'What went on back there?'

Both boys waited for the other to speak first. Jack didn't want to admit his behaviour, but then neither did Finn want to snitch on his friend.

'So?' the Captain insisted.

Finn reluctantly answered in a quiet voice.

'Jack was trying to get me to do something I didn't want to do.'

'Has this happened before?' asked the Captain.

'Yes,' Finn answered in an almost whisper.

The boys looked stubbornly at each other sideways.

'Listen up everyone,' said the Captain, sitting on the ground next to Finn. 'As you grow older, you'll all be faced with some challenging decisions, some of which don't have a clear right or wrong answer.'

He gestured for the girls to sit down.

'Some decisions are easy, like should I play soccer or rugby, netball or tennis. But other decisions involve asking yourselves more serious questions, like whether to cut class or do something you feel deep down inside, you really don't want to do.'

Finn avoided looking at Jack, worried that he would lay into him later for telling.

'What just happened boys, was a matter of your safety,' said Captain M. 'Making decisions on your own is hard enough, but when other people get involved and try to pressure you one way or another, it can become even harder.'

The Captain then went on to talk to the GeeBees about something called peer pressure.

'Your classmates are your peers and sometimes their influence can be positive, and you learn good things from each other. But other times it can be negative.'

'Like when they try to get you to do something you don't really want to do,' said Holly.

The Captain nodded a yes.

'It's normal to want to be liked and to feel you belong to a group of people,' he continued. 'But do you think it's possible to belong to a group without giving up who you are and what you believe?'

He looked directly at Finn and raised his eyebrows questioningly.

Finn shrugged his shoulders, not quite sure how to answer the question; but when the silence got too uncomfortable for him, he said out loud what was on his mind.

'But if I don't go along with him, then I'll be picked on even more.'

Isabelle immediately responded with a wise remark that surprised everyone, including herself.

'Well, maybe if he picks on you like that, then he's not really your friend.'

The Captain smiled at her and then looked back at Finn.

'You have to decide what feels right for you, Finn. Everyone has the right to express themselves and stand up for their point of view, as long as they respect the rights and beliefs of others.

You know that, right?'

Everything the Captain had said made sense.

'That's the way it should be, I guess,' said Finn.

'When you're able to do that, then you're being *assertive*. That means standing up for your rights without being pushy or just accepting something that feels wrong for you.'

'Jack was definitely being aggressive,' said Akira.

She couldn't help but take pleasure in watching Jack eat some humble pie.

'I didn't hit Finn or anything like that,' said Jack, in his own defence.

'*Aggressive* behaviour, Jack, isn't just about physical threats or actions,' said the Captain. 'It also includes verbal threats or actions - and it can be very hurtful.'

'You mean bullying,' said Akira.

She folded her arms across her chest and huffed at Jack.

'And gossiping behind your back,' added Isabelle.

The Captain nodded and said *'aha'*.

Everyone could see that Jack felt bad about his behaviour, even though he tried not to show it.

'You see Jack, if someone behaves aggressively, they are basically saying, "I say and do what I want without considering anyone else's feelings, as long as I get my own way."'

'Seems the tables have turned,' said Akira softly, but just loud enough for Jack to hear.

'On the other hand, avoiding the problem and letting someone be disrespectful to you isn't right either,' continued the Captain. 'That includes ignoring what's being said or done, without letting the other person know how you feel.'

'Like you're a pushover,' said Holly.

'That's called being *passive*,' said the Captain.

'Well, I always stand up for my rights,' Akira said.

Akira clearly had a healthy sense of self-worth and had no problems drawing the line, and saying 'no' when she wanted to.

'Always remember, it's important to respect the rights of other people,' said the Captain. 'But also respect yourself enough to let them know how you feel and what you want. That's what being assertive is all about.'

As he spoke, he took a token out from his pouch.

'This is for you Master Finn,' he said.

Finn immediately donned his most winning smile, and accepted the fourth token with pride.

'Vale Oria,' he said, reading the Hellenic words.

'Yes, Finn,' said the Captain. 'Draw the line and decide what feels right for you.'

Finn sprang to his feet and pushed his glasses back up to the bridge of his nose.

'I choose to be me,' he said loudly, holding his token in the air like a trophy.

7

SKIA STO NERO

*

SHADOW IN THE WATER

Finn's voice was clear and strong, ringing out with unusual power in the silent air. He had done the right thing by standing up for himself, and this had sown a seed that would soon grow and change how he dealt with any other challenge coming his way.

The Captain slapped Finn on the back.

'Five more Life Secrets to go,' he said, jovially.

'Let's go then,' said Finn.

Captain M led the GeeBees forward through another bamboo thicket until after a hundred yards or so, they finally reached the entrance to the Monster Caves. A dense barrier of undergrowth camouflaged the opening, which wasn't really very big.

'This looks a bit creepy,' said Holly.

She pulled back some hanging foliage to peer inside, but could see very little beyond the gloomy entrance. There was, however, something very strange and unearthly about the cave, which sent a shudder down her spine.

'I've heard so many stories of people going into caves like this and getting lost,' said Finn.

'You're kidding, right? asked Holly.

'No, I'm deadly serious.'

'I've heard that too,' said Jack. 'And most of them never make it out alive.'

'Oh, shut up, Jack,' said Akira.

'I'm not saying anything that's not true,' said Jack, on the defence.

'We'll all be together, so just stay close,' the Captain told them.

The Monster Caves consisted of a series of seven chambers, connected to each other by underground tubes and small passageways. Formed by water seeping into the ground over millions of years, these ancient caves had become the hideout for all sorts of unearthly creatures; ones that could only survive in the darkness.

'On this exploration, we'll only be going through two of the caves,' said the Captain.

'But how will we find our way in the dark,' said Akira, swallowing hard.

'Let's throw some light on the matter, shall we?'

Captain M pulled a chunk of vegetation to one side, entered the small opening, and grabbed a wooden torch from the wall sconce. The second he lit it, the flame was so bright it illuminated the entire entrance to the cave.

'Come on then,' he called out to the GeeBees.

No sooner had they all stepped in a few feet than a gust of wind kicked up, giving off a sound that resembled a distant howling of wild beasts. The gust swirled around and around everyone, like an invisible merry-go-round, until it stopped as suddenly as it had begun.

'*Whoa*, what was that?' said Isabelle.

'Did you feel that?' said Holly

'It was probably a ghost,' said Jack, very knowingly.

'Nothing of the sort,' answered the Captain.

'But there were voices,' Holly insisted.

'I heard them too,' said Akira.

'Yes, it sounded just like voices,' agreed Isabelle.

'That's why they call it the Aydoni singing tunnel,' said the Captain.

With no further explanation, he held the torch up high, revealing a passage with a rounded ceiling, coated in streaks of creamy-white calcite deposits. Black and terracotta-coloured paintings of ceremonial dances and hunting scenes, covered most of the wall surfaces.

As the explorers made their way down the passage, the images around them gradually began to come alive in the flickering torch light. Long robes of large, winged deities, flowed freely. Black figures danced and somersaulted off bulls' backs. Woolly sheep and shaggy goats seem to leap from the walls in an effort to escape packs of growling wolves.

'It looks so real,' said Isabelle.

'Just like a film,' said Finn in a hushed voice.

'Look at them jump,' said Holly.

She ducked quickly, thinking an animal was jumping out at her.

'It could be some kind of trick,' said Akira.

'Of course, it's a trick. Someone's probably messing around with our heads,' said Jack, shotting a glance at the Captain.

'Even art has a heart and a soul,' was the Captain's only response.

But it didn't matter. The GeeBees were so engrossed in watching the scenes play out around them, that his cryptic comment flew right past them. Shuffling along the tunnel at a snail's pace, they were all mesmerised by stories unfolding before their very eyes; so alive, so real, taking them further and further into the long-lost past.

The passageway continued to bear right and then, as they rounded a bend it ended at a stone wall.

'*Haaa*, a dead end,' said Jack.

'What do we do now?' asked Holly.

'Things are not always what they seem to be,' said the Captain.

'Can't you just give us a straight answer?' Akira said, under her breath.

'No, the Captain's right. We can't go back, so there must be a way, somehow, to move forwards,' said Finn.

He walked up to the wall, put his hands against it and pressed, thinking perhaps he could push his way out.

'It's stuck. We can't get out this way, that's for sure.'

'Push harder,' Jack said.

'Don't tell me what to do,' said Finn.

'Yeah, you tell him,' said Akira.

Not really knowing what he was looking for, Finn continued to run his hands over the smooth surface, until he felt something wet, and pulled back.

'Oh, *ewww*,' he said, cringing.

'What is it?' said Holly, becoming all panicky.

'I don't know, it's something slimy.'

The Captain lifted the torch higher and it was only then that they were able to see dozens of markings, smeared all over it the wall.

'They're symbols of some kind,' said Akira.

'More like black smudges,' said Jack.

'They could even be instructions,' said Finn.

'*Whoa*,' gasped Isabelle.

'What - what - what is it?' said Holly.

'Those seriously look like handprints,' Isabelle said.

They all froze for a few moments.

'Wicked,' said Jack. 'Maybe someone tried to get past but couldn't, and they got trapped here, and then they suffocated to death,' said Jack, all in one breath.

'Shut up!' everyone yelled together.

'Wait, there are only four fingers here,' said Finn.

He placed her open palm against the black markings and there was, without a doubt, a missing finger.

'That's definitely not human.'

'Maybe there's an alien, rotting corpse somewhere around here,' said Jack. 'What a great place for a murder.'

'Jack, stop it,' shouted Akira.

As her voice bounced off the walls, the wind started up again, whistling and whirling through the tunnel. Isabelle's hair swirled around her face and as she pulled it behind her ears, her eyes focussed on a vertical crack, running down the right side of the stone wall.

'See that?' she said, her finger pointing to the gap.

'Oh yes, that means this could be a door,' said Finn.

He wiggled his fingers like a magician and pressed both hands against that side of the wall. But nothing happened.

'Let's all push,' said Akira.

'Yes, come on,' Jack added.

With all their might, the five GeeBees pushed against the slab, and soon enough it began to open, just wide enough for everyone to squeeze past. Once through, they found themselves in an enormous cave; with glistening rock formations, shaped like waterfalls and icicles, hanging threateningly from the ceiling.

The glow from the Captain's torch reflected off the giant damp stalagmites and stalactites, that were growing at odd angles around them.

'Can you imagine being stabbed by one of those,' said Jack.

'I think they're beautiful,' said Isabelle.

'I think it looks like a gloomy tomb,' said Akira.

'Let's stay close together,' said the Captain, 'and advance slowly.'

It was dark and cold. The air was stale, heavy and humid, making it more difficult to breathe normally.

'What a stink,' said Holly.

'Like something's rotting,' said Jack.

'Smells like … sulphur,' said Finn.

'You're right, sulphur dioxide,' said Akira.

She wrinkled her nose and gave Jack a dirty look.

'Did you just let off that gas bomb?'

'You know the rule. Whoever smelt it, dealt it,' he replied, with a huge, fake smile.

'You're sooo not funny, Jack,' said Akira.

Weaving in and out of a forest of pointed rocks sticking up from the ground, the group made their way down the centre of the cave. The faint sound of water, slowly dripping through the roof - *drip, drip, drip* - echoed throughout the cave.

'Something's sticking to my trainers,' said Holly.

'Yeah, mine too,' Finn said.

He stopped for a moment, trying to flick something off the

bottom of his soles.

'What is it?' asked Holly.

'I guess it's mud,' Finn replied.

'Does anyone else get the feeling we're being watched?' Jack whispered loudly.

His dark, chocolate eyes darted around the chamber, but it was too dark to make out anything.

'Like we're not alone,' said Isabelle.

Then, without warning, something dropped from the stony ceiling and landed on Jack's head.

'*Aggh*, get it off me,' he yelped.

He brushed at his hair frantically until whatever it was, fell to the ground.

'What? What is it?' said Holly.

'Was it a bird?' asked Finn.

'How should I know,' said Jack, gawking at the ground.

The thing that had fallen on Jack's head was now lying very, very still.

'Why isn't it moving?' asked Akira.

'Maybe it's dead, said Isabelle.

As the GeeBees homed in to get a closer look, the tiny black object burst into life and shot back up to the top of the cave. They all leapt back in surprise and automatically looked upwards.

It was only then that they realised, that the jagged roof of the cave was alive and wriggling with thousands of dark creatures.

'What the ...' said Holly.

Her knees went all jittery.

'Yee-ikes, bats!' exclaimed Finn.

'It's a bat cave,' said Jack.

In the arch above their heads, there were tens of thousands of tiny bats, hanging upside down.

'Gross, this isn't mud,' said Isabelle, scraping the sole of her boot against a stone. 'It's poop.'

'*Ewww*, bat poo,' said Holly.

They all let out a holler, their voices echoing from one end of the cave to the other. Within seconds, an avalanche of bats fell from the ceiling, taking flight in every direction. The flapping produced so much wind that the torch flame went out, leaving them in pitch blackness.

'*Aggghhh!*' they all screamed together.

Human yells and deafening bat screeches blended together as the GeeBees ducked, covering their heads with their arms. But the bats kept on whacking into them, in what seemed like a frenzied attack.

Finn quickly pulled out his cricket bat. Using all his cricket moves to defend himself, he swung crazily at the tiny creatures. It was virtually impossible to hit what he couldn't see, but then a loud whomp sound told him that he'd got one.

Icky wet spray spewed everywhere.

'*Blaaah,*' said Jack, frantically wiping sticky goo from his lips and eyes.

'*Eww*, bat juice,' screamed Holly.

The chaos seemed to go on and on, until a deep booming voice suddenly called out, 'Papse, arketa.'

The Captain's angry rebuke rang through the cave, and sent the bats swarming back towards the ceiling. In no time at all, the sound of beating wings grew fainter and fainter, until the only thing that could be heard was the distant sound of running water.

A tense silence followed for a few moments.

'*Fttt - yuk*,' said Jack, spitting the remnants of something from his mouth.

The second he did that, everyone broke into fits of nervous laughter.

'What did you say to them?' Isabelle asked the Captain.

'I just ordered them to stop.'

He then relit the fire torch as if nothing had happened, and ever so slowly, the group continued forwards. The farther they moved into the cave, the closer they got to a green phosphorous light emanating from the ground.

'You can see everything here,' said Isabelle looking up at her surroundings.

'It's like someone flipped on the light switch,' said Jack, still able to find his goofy sense of humour.

'Is that water?' said Akira.

'It's an underground river,' answered the Captain.

'Why is it green?' asked Jack.

'Because of all the fluorescent algae that live there,' said the Captain.

The underground river ran the whole width of the cave, entering from the right, and disappearing under the rocks to the left. It was anyone's guess how deep it was, but what was most unusual about it was the green liquid that flowed through.

'It looks like a swimming pool lit up at night,' said Jack.

'Yeah, really,' said Holly.

'What's a drawbridge doing over here' Finn said.

He was pointing to an upright wooden construction, on the other side of the chasm.

'This must be some kind of moat,' said Akira.

'A moat and a drawbridge, without a castle - that doesn't make much sense,' said Jack.

'Well, it's definitely a drawbridge,' Akira snapped back at him.

'Why is it pulled up?' said Jack.

'You mean raised,' said Akira.

They gave each other a hard stare with narrowed eyes.

'Look, there's steps leading up from the water on this side - but not on the other,' said Finn.

'*Hmm*, let me think,' Akira mumbled, scratching her head.

'Obviously, the only way to get across then is to lower it somehow,' said Jack.

'But how? It's there and we're here,' Holly said.

'I guess, someone's got to jump across and let it down,' said Isabelle.

While this was going on, the Captain stood quietly in the background, listening and waiting for the GeeBees to come up with their own solution to the problem.

'Who in their right mind would volunteer to jump that,' said Akira.

She stood back, hands on her hips, looking down into the green murky water. For a few moments, everyone did exactly the same.

No one volunteered and they all stood in silence.

'Does anyone want to do it?' said Isabelle.

Still, no one spoke.

'It seems that I am the only one brave enough to accept the challenge,' said Jack, boldly.

He thrust his chest out in a quick and forceful motion. Jack didn't consider himself very agile, but he did have the advantage of height. Long legs were always a good thing for long jump. And more importantly, he relished the idea of being the hero of the day.

Everyone sighed a sigh of relief.

Jack walked along the edge of the river, inspecting possible points he could leap from, and generally making himself look very important. Swirling ripples just under the water's surface, suddenly caught his eye; a moving shadow appearing and disappearing in a matter of seconds.

'Did you see that?' he said, standing back.

'No, what?' said Finn.

Jack stood there for a moment looking down into the water.

'But there was a shadow – and a long one at that,' said Jack.

'I didn't see anything,' said Isabelle.

'Clearly a figment of your imagination,' said Akira.

Jack looked down again, but now there was nothing but slowly running water. Thoughts began to race through his head, and he imagined himself furiously treading water, kicking his legs fast and hard, fighting off a multi-tentacled monstrosity.

'I don't think my legs are strong enough to get a good running start,' he said, looking towards the Captain.

It seemed only wise to back out now while there was still time.

'I think those legs will give you all the push you need,' said the Captain.

'You can do it, Jack,' said Holly.

'Go for it, mate,' said Finn.

Jack swallowed hard, knowing he couldn't really go back on his word without feeling like an idiot. He was stuck between a rock and a hard place, and there was nothing he could do about it.

He took a few steps back to get a running start, and as he did this, all he could think about was flunking the jump.

'You're not going to make it,' chimed a voice in his head.

Jack's legs started to tremble, his breathing began to speed up, and he could feel his strength slowly draining away.

Licking his lips, Jack wiped his sweaty palms on his thighs and started to sprint; faster and faster until a few inches from the chasm, he jettisoned himself into the air. With his arms wind milling and his legs moving frantically out of control, Jack looked as if he had been hurled out of an ejection seat.

'He's not going to make it,' yelled Akira.

'Yes, he is,' said Isabelle.

Then, to everyone's horror, as Jack was in mid-air a scaly creature with fiery red eyes, leapt out of the water. With the force of a cyclone, it beat its green, leathery wings against the air, and caught hold of Jack with its mighty claws.

A savage shriek erupted from the monster's mouth as it dropped back into the water, disappearing with Jack into the depths of the river.

'Jaaaack!' everyone screamed.

'Help him,' shouted Holly.

'Do something,' Akira hollered to the Captain.

Running to the river's edge, the four of them threw themselves flat on their bellies, peering over the precipice.

'Can you see him anywhere?' asked Isabelle.

'Is he dead?' cried Holly.

Her voice broke down, and tears started to pour down her face.

'He can't be,' replied Akira.

Even Akira was desperate for Jack to appear.

Then, a few moments later, Isabelle pointed to a shadow and said, 'Look over there.'

'Yesss, it's him,' Finn said, with enthusiasm.

Jack had managed to fight his way to the surface, coughing

and spluttering. Splashing aimlessly and almost blinded by the water, he had no idea what had hit him.

'Grab my hand,' Finn called out.

'Swim faster,' Holly howled.

'Where?' called out Jack in panic. 'I can't see.'

'Over here,' Finn shouted back at him.

Splash - splash - splash, Jack waded his way through the water. But as he almost touched Finn's outstretched hand, he felt something tugging at his right leg.

'Nooo, it's got meeee!' he screamed.

Jack fought and struggled, barely able to keep his head above the water line. But his weak body was no match for the strength of the beast, as it started pulling him down.

And just as he was ready to let out his last breath, Jack felt something pulling at him from above. Captain M had come to the rescue. Plunging his arm into the water like a crane, he lifted Jack out and set him safely on the ground. He turned Jack onto his side, patting his back as he coughed up the clammy, green mucous.

Akira was the first to rush to Jack's side.

'Are you okay?' she said, falling on her knees.

Slowly coming to his senses, Jack propped himself up on his elbow and looked at Akira.

'So - *cough, cough,* - you do care after all,' he said, managing a choked chuckle.

Akira laughed out loud and said, 'Maybe, just a little bit.'

'Was that a dragon?' Finn asked the Captain.

'Yes, it was. One of the many Mind Monsters that inhabit the caves,' said the Captain.

'Mind Monsters!' exclaimed Holly.

'What are they?' asked Isabelle.

'*Ahhh,*' the Captain began, taking a deep breath. 'Mind Monsters are the negative thoughts, that we all battle with from time to time. They are the shadows that hover in the corner of our minds, feeding on our insecurities, worries and fears.'

'They don't sound very nice,' said Holly.

'Or look very nice,' said Akira.

'Mind Monsters, have been striking fear into human hearts, ever since the beginning of time; always trying to get our attention, commenting on everything that we do and feel,' the Captain continued.

'So, there's more than just this one?' said Akira.

She looked around slowly, warily, as if she was in real danger.

'Oh, yes indeed there are,' said the Captain. 'There's Thimos, the Anger monster; Anhos, the Worry monster; Erinios, the Guilt monster and many others too. The feisty creature you just met now was Apotihia, the Monster of Failure,' said the Captain.

'But it came out of nowhere,' said Finn.

'*Ahhh*, Mind Monsters can appear in the blink of an eye and when you least expect them.'

'But it was so real. How did it get here?' said Jack. 'And why did it pick on me?'

'Apotihia, is actually a "she" monster,' said the Captain, smiling. 'And she appears when anyone is worried about failing or making a mistake. And like the other Mind Monsters, Apotihia can appear from everywhere and nowhere all at once.'

'I can feel it coming,' said Isabelle.

'What, the monster?' Jack said, jumping to his feet.

'No …' said Isabelle trying to smother her giggle, 'I mean the next Life Secret.'

The Captain smiled and continued his explanation.

'You see, people often believe that trying something and risking possible failure, is a bad thing. So, they end up either never trying, or are often so focussed on failing or making a mistake, that that's what ends up happening.'

'Like when someone says, I can't,' Isabelle added.

'That's right, Izzy,' Captain M responded. 'And as we've said before, if you think you can't then you'll probably end up proving yourself right.'

Jack thought back to the last few moments before he made the jump.

'I really thought I wouldn't make it,' he admitted.

The Captain gave one of his all-knowing nods.

'Here's the important thing to remember, though. It's actually good to try something, even if it you don't get it right.'

Captain M commended Jack for trying, reassuring him that in so many ways, his failed attempt was a positive experience.

'Because, it's now given you a chance to learn how to do it right the next time.'

'You're saying that it's okay to make mistakes?' said Jack, scrunching up his face.

'Of course, everyone makes mistakes,' said the Captain, chuckling.

'What? Even grown-ups?' said Holly.

'Even us grown-ups,' said the Captain, chuckling. 'But every time you fall down after trying something, you will get up much stronger, and more prepared for the next time.'

'What do you mean?' asked Isabelle.

'Making a mistake is a valuable lesson, and it's how we learn,' he told them all.

'Sort of - like a chance to start over again,' said Finn.

'Exactly, Finn. Look at it as an opportunity to get it right and improve yourself. We most often learn by doing the wrong thing many times, before we find out the right way of doing it. And in order to get on in life and succeed, it's important that we have such experiences.'

'Basically, what you're saying is, that it's good to make mistakes,' said Jack, double-checking.

He had always believed that you had to get things right the first-time round.

'Yes, Jack. I call them learning opportunities in disguise.'

'But what happens if we don't learn from our mistakes?' said Holly.

She recalled all the times she had repeated the same mistake over and over again.

'There's only real failure, when you give up on something, or never learn from it.'

The Captain took a step to one side, and with his hand beckoned Jack to try the jump again.

'Remember, Apotihia only came to life and grew into a big monster, because you allowed her to.'

Jack pondered for a while, but it didn't take him long to realise that he wasn't ready to give up; not by a long shot.

'I get to say whether she stays or goes?' he said, boldly.

'You certainly do,' said the Captain.

Walking to the edge of the chasm, Jack looked into the water in search of a shadow, but there was nothing there.

'Second chance, right?' he said to the Captain.

'That's right, Jack. Learn from your experience and move on.'

With a little fine-tuning, and some help from his friends, Jack now felt more confident about undertaking the jump. Holly started coaching him about the importance of controlling his speed, when to jump and how to propel himself in air.

'Don't flap your arms and legs like you did before,' she said.

'It'll just increase your body drag,' added Finn.

'Really?' said Jack.

He didn't have a clue as to what went wrong when he jumped before.

'And remember, your body weight needs to be over the forward foot when you jump,' Holly said.

Isabelle reminded Jack to focus on his deep breathing, as she knew that this would help him calm down.

'It's effiktable,' she said.

Even Akira had something nice to say to Jack.

'Even though I think you're an idiot, I also know that if anyone can do this, you can.'

Jack didn't say much of anything and just nodded at his friends.

'Right, let's do it,' he said.

He drew in a deep long breath, then took a few more steps backwards, to get a good running start.

'If you think you can, then you will,' Isabelle reminded him.

Jack took in a few more deep breaths. He wasn't going to let Apotihia get the better of him again.

'Choose a target on the other side and keep your eye on it,' were the Captain's final words of advice.

Gritting his teeth, Jack looked past the ravine, to just beyond the drawbridge. As he did so, it became clear to him that the only obstacle between him and the other side was himself and his imagined Mind Monster.

After a fast run-up, he took three huge strides and pushed his feet into the ground, with full force. His body took off by itself, and he shot into the air like a spring. He flew over the chasm with such force and tumbled headfirst, as he landed on the other side.

'Hooray, he cleared it,' shouted Finn.

'Yay,' cried out Holly.

Jack caught his breath and turned towards his friends, smiling triumphantly. As everyone joined in with a round of cheers and applause, Jack beamed and took a long bow.

'Let down the drawbridge,' the Captain called out.

Jack unhooked the chains from the side posts, and slowly let the drawbridge down. One by one, the explorers crossed over the creaking planks. The green ooze below them bubbled and popped in a few places, but nothing more. No Apotihia. She had gone.

As Captain M passed over the bridge, he put a hand on Jack's shoulder.

'Well done my boy,' he said, putting the fifth token in his hand.

Jack felt a huge sense of pride, as he looked at the image of Apotihia, the Shadow in the Water.

'Skia sto Nero,' he read the Hellenic words out loud.

'We can't all be winners first time round,' the Captain said, addressing all the GeeBees. 'But Jack just showed us that a seeming failure, can clearly be turned into success.'

The group then walked up a slight rocky rise that looked like a small hill and into another cave. Not even close in size to the Aydoni singing cave, this one was smaller and rounder. But more astounding was the wide gaping hole above them.

It was as if the roof of the cave had been blown wide open by some mysterious force.

8

Right from the very first moment, it was plain that this was no ordinary cave. Most of the ceiling was missing and the surrounding stone wall was almost black, melted to a smooth finish by some form of extraordinary heat.

Smack dab in the middle stood a huge, twisted tree, riddled with gaps and hollows, rising up high into the night sky. Creeping up its broad trunk were several climbing vines, that welded together all the way to the top.

'Where are we?' said Isabelle.

'This is Ifestion Cave,' answered the Captain.

'But, it's not a cave,' said Finn, staring up at the hole above their heads.

'It was a cave, but is no longer!' said the Captain, laughing. 'It blew its top off a long, long time ago.'

A few seconds ticked by.

'Oh, I get it, it's a volcano,' said Finn.

'*Whoa*, we're in a volcano crater,' said Isabelle.

'According to legend, it was the eruption of Ifestion Cave that destroyed Andria.'

'If this is a volcano, that means …' said Jack.

'Don't worry, nothing's rumbled for thousands of years,' said the Captain.

'But it could still erupt,' said Jack.

'It's obviously extinct,' said Akira, sharply.

Her tone, however, didn't seem to faze Jack one bit.

'Yeah, but it could just be dormant,' he insisted.

'If the volcano was still alive then a tree this old wouldn't be here,' said Isabelle.

'Izzy's got a point,' said Holly.

'I guess that makes sense,' said Jack, feeling more reassured.

The tree really did look old, its massive trunk bigger than anything they had ever seen before. The starry sky above them provided enough light for them to see six hammocks, hanging like long cradles from the thick branches of the tree.

'I don't know about you lot, but I'm ready to drop,' said Finn.

He made a beeline for the nearest hammock and flopped into it, swinging like a monkey swaying from tree to tree.

'Me too,' said Holly.

Without another word she and the others followed suit, settling themselves into their hammocks for the night. It didn't take long for their breathing to quickly deepen as the gentle rocking of their hanging beds sent them all into a deep sleep.

Nine hours passed, before Isabelle woke up to the whisper of a soft, early morning breeze. She tried to open her eyes, but they were too heavy, too reluctant to open. But her mind was already awake, so she just lounged, taking in all the sounds around her; the humming, fluttering and buzzing sounds of tiny insects as they began their day.

Screwing up her face, Isabelle cracked one eye partially open, peeping at her surroundings. The sunlight glimmered through the spaces of the huge leaves above her, dancing over her eye and making it water.

Isabelle sniffed the air and couldn't smell the usual tell-tale smell of sulphur dioxide. In fact, here wasn't even so much as a smoulder to suggest they were in a volcano.

'Yep, it's definitely snuffed out,' she thought to herself.

Rubbing the sleep from her eyes, she looked around for the Captain's friendly face but quickly realised he wasn't there. Rolling onto her side, Isabelle carefully edged out of her hammock.

'Akira,' she said in a hushed voice.

Akira stirred slightly, but didn't wake up. Isabelle jostled her hammock.

'Get up, Akira.'

'What do you want?' Akira grumbled, sleepily.

'What's up?' said Finn.

He stretched his arms out, then looked at Isabelle with half-closed eyes.

'*Awww*,' said Holly, yawning loudly.

'Wake up. Come on, wake up,' insisted Isabelle.

Jack made a *pfff* sound with his mouth and turned over onto his other side.

'He's not here,' said Isabelle, with real concern in her voice.

'What is it?' asked Finn.

He sat up, rubbing his eyes, trying to focus on what Isabelle was saying.

'Captain M's gone.'

'Gone where?' said Holly.

'How should I know?' said Isabelle.

'But, why?' said Holly.

She couldn't understand why he would leave them all alone.

'There must be a reason,' said Isabelle.

'But he didn't say anything to us yesterday,' said Akira.

'He wouldn't just leave us here, would he?' said Finn.

He scanned left and right, but there was no sign of the trusted Captain.

'What are we going to do here on our own?' said Akira.

The thought of being left behind by the only person that could guide them to safety, left her feeling scared and annoyed.

'He can't have vanished into thin air,' said Finn.

'I've looked, but he's nowhere,' answered Isabelle.

Finn also didn't like being left in the lurch. Even though he had only known Captain M for a short time, he had bonded with him, and didn't mind admitting that he now felt a sense of abandonment.

Meanwhile, Jack lay snug in his hammock listening silently to every single word. Not sure how to react to the turn of events, he simply stuck his head under his pillow like an ostrich, and pretended that he was still asleep.

'What happens if we're stuck here forever?' said Holly.

Her voice had lost its usual cheerful ring, as it slowly dawned on her that she might never see her parents again.

It was as if a spell had been cast on the GeeBees. Their thoughts started to become cloudier and cloudier, until the fear of the unknown began to engulf them completely.

All except for Isabelle, that is. She was the only one who seemed able to remain calm. The words 'shift your focus' played in her head, as she remembered the importance of focussing on the positives in any situation.

'Maybe this has something to do with the next secret,' she said, with a glimmer of hope.

'But why would he go without even leaving us a message?' asked Akira.

'Message?' said Isabelle. '*Hmmm*, maybe he did just that.'

Taking stock of her surroundings, Isabelle noticed something that looked like a dried leaf on the tree trunk.

'What's that?' she said.

'It looks like a scroll,' said Holly.

'It is – it's a paper scroll.'

Isabelle pulled the object from behind a thin strip of peeling bark. She carefully untied the fine string from around the scroll, and rolled it on her open palm to flatten it.

'Well?' said Akira, impatiently.

'Is it from the Captain?' said Finn.

'I think so,' said Isabelle, scanning the hand-written document.

'What does it say?' said Jack.

'Finally, you've joined us,' said Akira.

Isabelle told them to listen up and started reading the message out loud.

To find out Life Secret Number Six,
Look for something that resembles a candlestick,
Something that has a neck but no feet,
Something that will help you take a great leap.

'Oh, goody - a riddle,' said Holly, excitedly.

Jack reached out from his hammock and snatched the paper from Isabelle's hand.

'Hey, we were reading that,' Holly reacted.

'You need a brain to solve this one,' said Jack, smugly.

A few seconds passed and then he threw the paper back at Isabelle saying,

'Yes, I can confirm, it's a riddle.'

Akira sighed heavily and tutted.

'You're such an idiot.'

'I knew this had something to do with the next secret,' said Isabelle.

In spite of this clue, Isabelle was still the only one that could see something good in all of this situation. The others kept their attention on the negative side of the Captain's disappearance.

'I don't think this is the time for stupid games,' Akira said, folding her arms defensively.

'I still can't understand why he left us alone,' said Finn.

'What's going to happen to us? What happens if one of those monsters comes and gets us?' said Holly.

'Whatever,' sighed Jack.

He turned his back towards everyone and nestled himself comfortably into his hammock once again.

Five completely different reactions to the turn of events; anger, fear, disappointment, denial and hope. It was as if the GeeBees were running together in a pack, feeding off of each other's reactions.

'Hey, come on you lot,' Isabelle said, in a raised voice. 'Stop focussing on us being stuck here, and let's work out how we can get out of this mess.'

For a moment, everyone stared at Isabelle, stunned at her outburst. They'd never heard her speak with such firmness.

'Izzy's right. We have to stick together,' said Akira, eager to show off her superiority.

The five of them agreed, half-heartedly albeit, to keep a positive attitude, and began to scour every inch of the crater;

looking for something that had a neck but no feet.

After a while of searching, Finn noticed a small arched niche sunk into the wall. On it stood a black object, much the same colour and texture as the walls surrounding it.

'Is that a bottle?' he said.

'I think it could be,' said Holly.

'The message said something like a candlestick,' said Isabelle.

'That must be it, a bottle has a neck but no feet,' Akira said.

Finn picked the elongated bottle off the shelf, and held it up in the air as if it was a trophy.

'A message in a bottle - how original,' said Jack, still lounging in his hammock.

'Who asked your opinion?' said Akira. 'You haven't lifted a finger to help out.'

'This is all such fun,' said Isabelle, shuddering with excitement.

Finn automatically handed the bottle to Isabelle, as if she was the team leader.

'You do it,' he said.

And so, Isabelle popped open the cork top and pulled out a thick roll of paper from inside, reading the message.

When I know, I'm in control,

When I don't, it might take over.

Which mind monster is coming closer?'

The GeeBees brooded over the riddle, coming up with this and that and toying with lots of ideas. A few minutes passed when Akira said,

'Eureka!'

'What's eureka?' said Jack.

'*Derr* - it means I found it.'

'What's the answer, then?' said Holly.

'The unknown,' said Akira, with certainty. 'It's the Monster of the Unknown.'

'What does that mean?' said Isabelle.

'Well …' Akira started to explain.

'And how did you work that one out, missy clever pants?' said Jack

'Just leave this one to me Jack,' replied Akira, without hesitation. 'You can work out the riddle to the Monster of Stupidity.'

Jack opened his mouth to speak, but couldn't hit back with an equally sharp reply. So, he just huffed sarcastically.

'So, the unknown, like what we're facing now,' said Finn.

'Yes, think about it. When I know something, then I'm more in control of my reactions. And when I don't know what I'm facing - like something new - then my fear takes over.'

'Oh, I see,' said Isabelle. 'When you don't know something, it means it's the unknown. And if you're scared of it, then the monster will appear.'

'You're right, Akira,' said Finn.

'I always am.'

She looked at everyone, smiling smugly as if she'd just won the prize for greatness.

Everything was finally beginning to make sense. The explorers were facing a difficult transition into the unknown. Being left on their own, in a new situation that they believed they weren't ready for, had left most of them feeling scared and vulnerable.

'So, we're being tested somehow,' said Isabelle.

'Yes, that's right,' said Akira.

Both girls spoke with equal determination but without being really sure where all this was leading.

'So, that means that there's another …' Finn said.

The words remained locked in his mouth.

At that very moment, a massive misty mass began to creep across the volcano opening, casting a sinister shadow over the ground below.

'Is that a cloud?' said Holly.

'I hope it's not going to rain,' said Akira.

'It looks more like something foggy,' said Isabelle.

At that moment, the shadow above them released a deep, rumbling sound.

'No amount of wishful thinking is going to make that thing a cloud,' Jack said.

He leapt out of his hammock and took cover, as the mist began to break up, revealing a dragon the size of a fighter jet. The creature was dark and massive, its eyes fiery red and scales sparkling a crimson purple. It circled above them, beating its leathery wings hard, and then lowered its head to give them a deathly glare.

'Oh nooo, it's staring at us,' whimpered Holly.

'Look at those massive claws,' said Finn.

'It'll grab one of us,' Akira whimpered.

She was so terrified she didn't know if she should move, or even where to go.

The dragon drew back its blotched gums, displaying a multitude of razor-sharp teeth. Opening its jaws even wider, it forcefully exhaled a torrent of smelly breath.

'Fovou to agnosto,' were the blood-curdling words that spilled from its mouth.

'What did it say?' screamed Holly.

'Fear the unknown,' Akira said.

And so, the stage was being set for the GeeBees to fight

off their final Mind Monster; Agnosto, the Monster of the Unknown.

'Quick, hide,' yelled Jack, squeezing into a large hollow of the tree.

Finn dropped down on the ground and rolled over to the safety of some undergrowth, whilst Holly dived for cover under her hammock. Akira flattened herself against the wall, hoping her black hair and dark uniform would provide the camouflage she needed.

'Hide Izzy,' cried out Holly.

Unlike the others, Isabelle stood her ground, without flinching. An inexplicable feeling of confidence surged through her body, like an electrical current. It's not that she wasn't scared of the monster's ferociousness, because she was. But Isabelle's logic was somehow stronger than her emotion, and this helped her keep a cool head.

'It's not real, it's not real,' she repeated over and over again.

Agnosto gave off another ear-deafening screech that split the air like thunder.

'Erhome na se fao,' he blasted at her.

'Izzy, he says he's going to eat you,' screamed Akira, at the top of her lungs.

'I know, I heard,' Isabelle cried back.

'Get out of the way,' said Holly in a wild panic.

But Isabelle still did not move an inch. Somewhere, deep inside her, she knew that it was her destiny to conquer this Monster of the Unknown. She had to at least try to be what she was - the actress she always wanted to be, and like a heroine, act her part out to its full.

While Agnosto gnashed his teeth in rage, Isabelle heard a *tinkle - tinkle - ting-a-ling* sound from deep inside her, telling her to trust her instinct and to keep on doing what she was doing.

'Let's finish this,' she said, with a determined look on her face.

Isabelle stared up defiantly at the great dragon looming over her. As it met her gaze, she reached deep inside for all her power. Swallowing hard, she stretched her arm towards the monster, as if she were holding an invincible sword.

'Papse, siopee, den fovame,' she cried out.

Isabelle repeated the words (stop, silence, I'm not afraid) several times like a chant, with an ever-increasing air of authority. She clapped her hands three times - *clap, clap, clap* - and repeated the Hellenic words once again.

'Papse, siopee, den fovame,' she said, this time even more defiantly.

As she spoke Agnosto slowly began to spin, gradually picking up speed until he was spinning wildly and almost out of control. Then, like a missile firing, he went whoosh, shooting high into the sky and vanishing into thin air.

All Isabelle could hear was the sound of her own heartbeat thumping in her chest. It was so loud she was sure everyone could hear it. Still just about standing, she shuffled backwards and looked up at the sky with disbelief. She took a huge breath that swelled in her chest and let it out with a long '*whoaaa*'.

Akira, Holly, Jack and Finn all came out of their hiding places, bursting into chatter and laughter.

'You saved us,' Holly said.

She jumped up and down on her tiptoes, clapping with excitement.

'I don't think I could ever have done what you just did,' said Akira.

'You were totally awesome,' said Finn, playfully punching

Isabelle in the shoulder.

This was the first time that Isabelle had ever felt such a tremendous power being unleashed from within her; a strong inner humming energy, that was growing stronger and stronger by the day.

Still in shock, she just stood there and stared.

'You can be on my team any day,' chortled Jack.

'Too late, she's with me,' responded Akira, looping her arm around Isabelle's neck.

They all burst out laughing once again, with the sort of nervous laughter that was mixed with relief.

'Do you think the monster's completely gone?' asked Holly.

'Yes, if he was ever really here in the first place,' said Isabelle.

A voice called out from above them.

'The old is gone and the new has come.'

'Captain M,' squealed Holly.

The GeeBees could barely contain their excitement, as they saw their guide peering over the rim of the volcano.

'Isabelle saved us,' called up Finn.

'She took the monster on all by herself,' said Akira.

The Captain listened, as they all talked and laughed incessantly about Isabelle's greatest performance.

'I guess anything is effiktable if you really believe it is,' said Isabelle, smiling.

'*Yaaayyy*,' Akira and Holly said together.

'Are you all planning to stay down there all day?' said the Captain, jovially.

'No way,' said Holly, making her way to the tree.

'Wait,' said Akira, stopping Holly in her tracks. 'I think Izzy should go first.'

Isabelle's cheeks flushed. She considered Akira not only a

friend but a natural leader. So, to be told by her that she should be up front, was a sign of great reverence.

'Thank you,' she said.

'We thank you,' responded Akira, with a warm smile.

Isabelle had never climbed a tree before, and she didn't know if she could.

'If Agnosto can't stop me, then a tree certainly won't,' she thought to herself.

And so, she pulled herself up by swinging her legs and wrapping them around the first big branch. Then the next branch and then the next, climbing higher and higher until from the top branches she could almost touch the stone rim.

'Grab my hand,' said the Captain.

In one swoop he hauled her up and over the edge of the volcano. In turn, the GeeBees followed her lead, weaving their way through the tangle of branches twigs and leaves.

Isabelle glanced back down one more time into the crater. This had been one of the greatest trials of her life. What made it even greater was the fact that, only two days ago, she would never have even thought of facing such a monster head on. Yet now, she had never considered giving up; not for one moment.

Turning to the Captain she said,

'So, the secret is about how we handle the unknown?'

'Yes, Izzy,' he replied. 'It's about the changes that happen in our lives and our response to the unknown that it brings with it.'

Captain M sat down cross-legged, and patted the ground beside him, signalling the explorers to sit as well.

'We all face changes every single day of our lives, and we all have to walk into the unknown at one time or another,' he told them.

'We've been through plenty of changes since we got here,' said Akira.

'We sure have,' said Finn.

Captain M smiled and nodded.

'Handling those changes isn't always easy, is it?'

'No, it isn't,' said Isabelle.

She immediately thought about her new life at boarding school.

'Well, sometimes it is and sometimes it isn't,' said Akira, with an air of worldly wisdom.

'Exactly Akira,' responded the Captain. 'Each person deals with those changes differently.'

For some people, he told them, it was harder than for others.

'Some people can go through change and flow, adapting as if nothing much has happened. Whilst other people can feel scared, worried, sad or angry about the change,' he said.

He paused for a few moments, leaving them all time to ponder.

'Kind of like the way we all reacted before?' said Jack, realising that he had dealt with everything in the cave with denial.

'Yes Jack,' said the Captain.

He then went on to talk to the GeeBees about the types of changes that they would undoubtedly face in their lives; expected or unexpected, wanted or unwanted.

'On the one hand, there are the changes that we feel we have a choice about, that we want to happen or that we are excited about,' said Captain M.

'Like Max being born,' said Holly, referring to her baby brother.

'And when we moved to a bigger house,' Akira said, happy

to have her own bedroom at last.

The Captain nodded and smiled.

'We're all enthusiastic about these types of changes. because we believe they will make our life better in some way,' he said.

Again, the Captain paused, giving them time to register his words.

'But when we are uncertain about the change - if something happens without our choice or without warning, then those changes tend to leave us feeling scared.'

'And probably not so happy,' said Finn.

'Exactly,' said the Captain.

'Like being forced to change schools,' was Isabelle's first thought.

'When my dad lost his job, we had to move home,' said Holly.

The Captain gave another of his characteristic nods.

'Now, some people can deal with these changes just fine,' he said, 'but most times, these unexpected changes can leave us feeling sad, scared, angry or even in denial.'

'So, that's why the Monster of Change showed up before,' Finn realised.

'He could smell all of us being scared of what was going to happen,' Jack added in a spooky voice.

Captain M nodded once again.

'But here's the thing, it's important to realise that any type of change also brings opportunities with it. Think about it … in order to have something new or different, something has to change,' he said.

'That makes sense,' said Akira.

'I guess so,' said Holly.

'Just like the day and night, or the wind that blows, change is an inevitable part of life,' he continued. 'The problem is, if you are fearful of the change, then the fear can often blind you, or keep you stuck where you are. And that way, you end up by focussing on the fear, and not on finding a solution. You just can't see all the opportunities and possibilities that are passing you by.

'So, that's when we should shift our focus and look at the bright side of things,' said Isabelle.

'Precisely so,' said the Captain.

His features brightened as he took out his leather pouch. He removed the sixth token, with the words Winds of Change etched on it, and gave it to Isabelle.

'Anemi tis Allagis,' she mouthed the words.

'And now,' the Captain said, 'it's time for more change.'

He stood up, dusted the dirt off his clothes and started walking down the hillside, with the GeeBees following close behind.

Waiting for them at the foot of the knoll was a wave of gently nodding faces.

'*Ha ha haaa* - greetings,' said the Captain, swinging out his arms, his fingers opened and spread.

AVATON TOWERS

9

FOS ODIGOS
*
GUIDING LIGHT

There was an explosion of cheers and happy laughter as dozens of dwarfish humans surrounded the explorers, exchanging handshakes and slaps on the back. Standing barely over four feet in height, they were all quite similar in appearance. They had dumpy, stout bodies like well-padded cushions and eyes that were a beautiful shade of turquoise, unlike any eyes the GeeBees had seen before.

'Welcome to Arnee. Please join us in celebration. A feast in your honour awaits,' said a little chap, with a ginger beard and chipmunk cheeks.

He led everyone down a path that gradually descended through the undergrowth towards Arnee, a hamlet nestled deep in the Avaton Forest beneath the Avaton Towers.

As they neared their destination, the air carried a faint but mouth-watering smell of food to everyone's nostrils. Jack's stomach growled emptily, as if it were smelling the enticing aroma.

'Sausages, bacon, scrambled eggs,' he said, sniffing the air as he walked.

'*Mmmm*, baked beans,' said Holly.

'I'm famished,' said Finn.

'Food, glorious food, cold jelly and custard,' Isabelle sang, swinging her arms like a conductor.

On arriving at the hamlet, the explorers were met with a very busy scene. Countless little bodies scurried around like commandos in a military operation, preparing a grand table full of food.

Their little guide slapped his hands together and quickly reeled off a list of instructions in Hellenic.

'*Whoa*, look at that,' said Isabelle, staring in disbelief at the mountain of food in front of them.

'Is it all for us?' asked Jack.

'All for you, all for you,' said a plumpish woman.

Sitting on a small wooden stool, she was peeling potatoes and placing them into a bucket at her feet.

'Sit down and eat,' said their guide.

Quick as a flash, the GeeBees took their places and tucked into the towering stack of blueberry pancakes, cream puffs, sandwiches and eggs Benedict.

'*Mmm*, this is good,' said Finn, swallowing a sweet, gooey juice in just a few enthusiastic gulps.

'Yummy,' said Holly.

She licked her fingers as if they were lollipops.

'Delectable,' Akira said, looking around to see what she could devour next.

'Delicious,' murmured Isabelle in between bites.

The atmosphere was charged with excitement as they

gobbled down as much food as they could, happy to feel full once again.

The leaves of the giant oaks above them glistened, changing colour as they shimmered and fluttered about in the early morning breeze.

'They look like …' Isabelle paused, squinting upwards at the sun's glare, 'hands waving at us.'

'Hello,' said Holly, waving back at them.

They both giggled.

'Can we have a look around?' asked Akira.

She was intrigued by the cluster of quaint, stone cottages all around her. Like a drawing from a fairy-tale book, all the little buildings had cute square-latticed windows and thatched roofs with straw peeping over their warped front doors.

'No time for that, I'm afraid - we've got to keep on moving,' was Captain M's reply.

'Oh but …' said Akira.

'No buts about it. We must reach the top of Avaton Tower before nightfall.'

At something less than twenty miles, their exploration on Aydagar was nearing its end, and they had a deadline to meet. And so, the GeeBees bid their farewells to the Arneeans, and set off deeper into the forest of vivid green firs, giant oaks and lofty cypress trees.

The first leg of the journey took them along a trail that rose gently through the thick forest, dipping down at times but mostly winding upwards. The deeper they entered the forest the more impenetrable the vegetation became. Gigantic branches above them twisted and intertwined with smaller trees, bushes and creepers, creating a green ceiling above them. This only allowed intermittent patches of white light to shine through.

'Awesome, it's like a secret tunnel,' said Finn, looking up at the thickly matted leaves above his head

'*Ouch*, that hurt,' said Akira, as a sharp pain shot up her ankle.

She had stumbled over a protruding root, hidden by a blanket of rotting leaves.

'I didn't touch her, I promise,' said Jack.

He took a deep breath and waited, looking at the Captain and then at Akira. He was sure she was going to say something. But she didn't. Akira just jumped to her feet and wiggled her ankle to make sure it was okay.

'*Phew*,' Jack sighed with relief.

'There's hundreds of them,' said Finn.

Pushing the leaves aside with his trainers, revealed multiple roots of different sizes, zigzagging across the ground.

'They look like snakes, don't they?' he said.

'More like bony alien fingers,' said Jack.

He grinned devilishly, but his remark was met with stony faces. No one was in the mood for more surprise visits from monsters or creatures of any kind.

The group continued along the winding path, until they came to an old wooden stile that guarded the entrance to another dense, leafy passage. Just beyond, was a flight of roughly hewn stone steps leading upwards, taking them out of the forest towards the two rock towers.

'Two, four ... sixteen ... twenty-two,' said Holly, counting.

Her feet hardly seemed to touch the ground as she gracefully sprang up the steps.

'*Oh*, not again,' said Akira.

She could never understand where Holly got all her energy from. Instead, she plodded slowly upwards, focussing on the carpet of moss and slippery lichens that covered the old stone slabs.

At this level of elevation, the dense forest had thinned considerably, opening out towards a large expanse of purple fields. The air was filled with the fragrance of the miniature wildflowers that stretched all the way to the base of the Avaton Towers.

'*Whoa*, that is - out of this world,' said Isabelle, gaping at the vast rock towers dominating the landscape in front of them.

'They're humungous,' said Finn.

'They look like the Darth Vader brothers,' Jack remarked, jokingly.

'Darth Vader hasn't got a brother,' said Akira.

'And you don't have a sense of humour.'

Their confrontation was short-lived, ending in Jack cupping his palm over his armpit and pumping his arm up and down. This made a sound identical to a wet sounding fart. Akira groaned with disgust.

The massive monoliths of smooth, windswept rock rose abruptly upward out of the ground, looming over them like two giants. Wrapped around the base of the soaring rock pinnacles was a low-hanging cloud, making it look as if the towers were suspended in mid-air.

Avaton Tower, with its chiselled face, was the largest of the two rock towers. Standing just next to it to the right, was the slightly smaller, more pyramid shaped anti-Avaton Tower.

'You expect us to climb that?' said Akira, giving the Captain one of her dubious looks.

'Yep, that's where we're aiming for.'

The Captain pointed to the very top of the larger rock tower.

'You've got to be kidding me,' Akira said.

'I kid not.'

'What's that up on the top?' asked Finn.

Perched on the summit of the Avaton Tower was a sanctuary, barely visible through the clouds.

'That, is the eternal temple in the sky,' said the Captain. 'It's a sacred place, where entry is restricted to only those who have undertaken an exploration such as this one.'

'You mean, the chosen few,' said Jack, smugly.

'Just so,' replied the Captain.

'That is so cool,' said Finn.

'I can't wait,' said Isabelle, grinning happily.

Akira gave her friend a disbelieving sideways glance, as if to say, 'are you crazy?'.

'It's going to be fabulous, Akira,' Isabelle said.

'If you say so,' Akira huffed.

'Well then - I say so!'

'But, how are we going to get there?' said Akira. 'It looks completely inaccessible.'

'Once we make our way through the fog and climb halfway up the anti-Avaton Tower,' the Captain said pointing upwards, 'then all we have to do next, is inch along that narrow rock ledge, cross the arch bridge and finally, scale that wall of rock in a wicker basket.'

The way he spoke, it was as if it would be the easiest thing in the world to do. Akira looked at the bare, vertical rockface on the Avaton Tower, and gave the Captain a shocked stare. She didn't have to say anything; her expression said it all.

'Come on Akira, we've made it this far, right?' said Holly, playfully nudging her friend with her elbow.

'So - far - you mean,' replied Akira.

'We're on the last leg of our journey,' said the Captain.

A fine veil of early morning mist hung heavily in the air,

giving everything a rather ghostly look.

'You're it,' said Holly, tapping Finn on the shoulder.

Finn started chasing her and soon they were all running around the purple field of flowers, laughing and playing a never-ending game of tag.

Captain M wandered over to the base of the shorter anti-Avaton Tower, where two massive lion statues guarded the entrance to the walkway. Defenders of the sacred Avaton Temple, the stone beasts stood in motionless obedience, their mouths in a wide-open roar.

The Captain picked up a curled ram's horn and held it to his lips. Drawing a deep breath, he blew a long, strident blast. Then another, and another. And one final longer blast, the sound resounding across the fields.

Well-rehearsed at responding to bells and signals, the GeeBees scurried towards him and assembled at the entry point to the tower. The mist here was thicker, slithering around their bodies like a prowling phantom.

'How are we going to make our way through this?' asked Jack, wafting his hand in front of his face.

'I can hardly see a thing in front of me,' Akira said.

It was very clear to her that they could easily get lost, or worse still, plunge from a great height towards a certain death.

'That light will keep us on track,' said the Captain.

'What light?' asked Finn.

'There,' replied Captain M, pointing upwards.

Just above the halfway point on the anti-Avaton tower, they could make out a faint, but unmistakable glow.

'Oh yes, over there,' said Holly.

'I still can't see anything,' said Jack.

'There,' said Akira, grabbing his chin and pointing him in

the right direction.

'Oh, you mean there,' said Jack, pushing her away.

'What is it?' asked Isabelle.

'That, my friends, is the Crystal Obelisk.'

The landmark he was referring to, was a massive upright pillar, carved from a single piece of crystal quartz. It had four sides that gradually tapered as it rose, seemingly terminating in an apex of a pyramid shape.

A light of hope in the darkness, the crystal obelisk had provided many travellers with a good sense of direction; guiding them safely through the menacing mists and storms, at the base of the towers.

'Is that where we have to get to?' asked Isabelle

'Yes, it's our first goal,' answered the Captain.

'So, are we going to play soccer then?' asked Jack, half in jest.

The only type of goal that came to his mind was the type that included a ball and a goal post.

'Clearly not,' said Akira with a biting tone. 'He's obviously talking about a target.'

'Why do we need a goal?' said Holly.

'Exactly my question to you,' responded the Captain. 'Why do we need to have a goal?'

'I guess it gives us something to aim for,' replied Finn.

'Exactly, Finn,' answered the Captain. 'Setting a goal allows you to know what you want, and where it is.'

In the case of this exploration, their final destination was Avaton Temple, so that was a very clear goal.

'Now, once we know our main goal, I always find it helpful to break that goal down into smaller mini-goals.'

Taking out an old map of Aydagar from his pocket, the

Captain continued his explanation.

'You see, mini-goals are a series of smaller steps you can take that will get you closer to your overall, big goal.'

The group came to a standstill, to look at the map and consider the steps, or milestones as the Captain also called them, that they needed to take in order to get to the temple.

Firstly, they would have to make their way through the fog and mist, to the narrow rock ledge called the Diavolo Drop. Once they had crossed that, they would move onto the Crystal Obelisk and then across the old stone bridge.

'All that's left after that, is the wicker basket that'll pull us up to Avaton Temple,' said the Captain.

'How long will that take?' said Akira.

'As long as it takes to get there - but we must have arrived by the time the radiant sun turns red,' he told them.

'Baskets and drops don't sound very safe to me,' said Akira.

'It'll be such fun, you'll see,' Holly said.

'So, that means we've got three mini-goals before we get to our big goal,' said Finn.

The Captain nodded and smiled.

With that sorted, the group set off, disappearing into the mist up the slope ahead. Previous rains had made the ground muddy and hard to walk on, so the GeeBees shunted forwards slowly, as if they were glued to one another. All that could be heard was the squelch of sludge under their feet, and the sound of their heels scuffing up little splats of mud.

Before long, the trail branched out in two directions. One fork, signposted Arkadia Falls led to the right, whilst the other fork would take them directly to their destination.

'Arkadia falls - is that far from here?' Holly said, excited about the idea of checking the place out.

The Captain informed her that by taking this right turn towards Arkadia, they would go off track and over to the other side of the Avaton Towers.

'We've no time for that now.'

'It sounds so nice. Falls - does that mean a waterfall?' said Holly. 'Please tell us something about the place.'

The Captain took out his pocket watch to check the time.

'Okay then, but quickly.'

He went on to speak about the unspoilt, harmonious wilderness of Arkadia, and the magical creatures that made it their home.

'The most illustrious inhabitants are the Aiads and Aryads.'

'Who are they?' said Isabelle.

'They're the lovely ladies of the trees and waters,' said the Captain.

'Ladies?' said Jack, one eyebrow rising.

'Well, more like spirits of nature.'

'You mean spirits, as in - not real?' said Akira.

'They are in fact very real, Akira, but just from a different dimension.'

Humanlike in appearance, these fairy-tale spirits, or nymphs as they were also known, lived together in the lush woods, waterfalls and streams on the far northern side of the island. With long, silky hair and snow-white skin, their beauty was said to be unlike anything anyone from the human world had seen before.

The Aryads were supernaturally connected to the trees they called home, fiercely watching over them at all times.

'These beautiful nymphs can make plants grow within seconds and can even transform a seed into a towering oak tree,' said the Captain.

'Is that for real?' Isabelle said, with a raised voice.

The Captain answered with a couple of '*ahaas*' and gave a light-hearted laugh.

'I vote we go there,' said Akira.

This sounded like a far nicer alternative to climbing the rock towers.

'Can we really go?' asked Holly, giggling excitedly.

But before the Captain could answer, Isabelle asked him about the Aiads.

'You didn't tell us about the Aiad nymphs.'

'Ah, yes,' said the Captain. 'Well, they guard the flowing waterfall and cool, bubbling streams of Arkadia. And as long as their home waters run strong, the Aiads will remain young, beautiful and vigorous.'

'And if something happens to the water?' said Holly.

'If the waters run low, their strength easily slips away from them.'

'Really?' said Holly.

The Captain nodded.

'The Aiads also have magical qualities. It is said, that if you wash in their waters, you can be healed of any sickness.'

Trembling with excitement at the prospect of meeting such exotic, magical creatures, Holly pleaded with the Captain.

'Please, can we just go and see them?'

'Oh, please, please,' implored Akira and Isabelle.

Overwhelmed with eagerness to go to Arkadia, the girls started jumping up and down on the spot; completely forgetting everything that they had previously discussed about reaching the Avaton Temple.

'If you choose to go there, it'll definitely be a wonderful experience …' replied the Captain.

'Yes, yes,' the girls said.

'But it'll take us away from our goal,' said Finn.

'Finn is absolutely right,' said the Captain in a more sombre voice.

He furrowed his brow in the centre between his eyebrows, and looked from Holly to Isabelle, and finally to Akira.

'Not only will we miss our target and deadline, but this will also involve a risk,' he told them.

'A risk!' Akira exclaimed.

'What risk?' asked Finn.

The Captain rubbed his beard with his hand and his eyes stared at the girls.

'The obelisk will only shine its light, as long as you focus on it. If your attention turns elsewhere, this will cause the light to fade.'

'That means we won't be able to find our way through this fog,' said Finn.

'Then we need to focus on the obelisk,' said Jack, as if he had made a decision. 'And stop thinking about stupid fairies and pixies.'

'As long as you focus on the obelisk, it will shine its light and show you the way,' the Captain reiterated.

'It's so gloomy here,' said Finn, 'we'll definitely lose our way without it.'

'And, we'll also lose valuable time,' added the Captain.

In essence, Arkadia was a distraction that would not only send them off track, but would prevent the GeeBees from reaching their goal by dark.

'You must all be present for the full moon ceremony,' the Captain told them.

'Full moon ceremony?' Isabelle repeated, with awe.

Images of ancient marble temples, and mysteriously veiled maidens clothed in white, silk robes flashed through her mind.

'So, what happens if we don't get there in time?' said Finn.

'The gates to the temple only open once a month for the ceremony,' the Captain said. 'All those who fail to reach that point by nightfall, will automatically be banished from the island.'

'N - o - o - o,' Finn said.

'That's not fair,' said Jack.

'Either you're in the temple by nightfall or you go home,' said the Captain.

'What, without getting to the best part?' Jack said.

'But we've come so far,' said Finn.

He was not at all pleased with the fact that, everything they had been through over the last couple of days, would have been for nothing.

The Captain was insistent.

'The rules of the game are simple - any explorer remaining outside the temple after the setting of the sun, on the last night of the exploration, will be removed from Aydagar.'

The GeeBees gasped in shock and surprise.

'And one more important thing - all the memories of all you have done here, will be wiped out.'

'You mean complete memory loss?' said Akira.

'No, that can't be,' Isabelle protested.

'That's insane,' said Jack.

The Captain nodded and made a little grimace. It was out of his hands. If they didn't reach the temple at the designated time, every single experience on Aydagar and all the secret tokens would be lost, forever.

Only the GeeBees who had journeyed all the way to Avaton

Temple, having gained all nine Life Secrets, had the right to attend the sacred Moon Ceremony, and keep their new-found knowledge forever.

'Whoever doesn't finish, doesn't remember,' said the Captain, in a very matter-of-fact way.

The five explorers remained silent for several moments, trying to digest what they had just heard.

'Well then, we clearly have to stay on track,' said Finn. 'There's only one way forward and it's to the left.'

'I agree,' said Isabelle. 'I don't want to go back to the way things were.'

After all, in just such a short time she had begun transforming from a shy girl, lacking in self-confidence into a more self-assured person.

'Neither do I,' said Finn, firmly.

For the first time, Finn had found the courage to say a big 'no' to something he was not comfortable doing. He certainly didn't want to give that up.

'Were you planning to just zap us if we didn't make it to the top?' Jack asked the Captain.

He laughed, but at the same time didn't want to let go of all that he had learnt. On Aydagar, Jack had realised that his real strength lay in being fair, and showing respect to those around him rather than being always loud or aggressive.

'But how can you undo what's been done?' asked Finn.

'Yeah, how can you unlearn something once it's been learnt?' said Akira.

'It doesn't matter. The point is, we need to head for the obelisk,' said Finn.

Captain M had already pulled the seventh token from his pouch and held it out to Finn.

'Well done, Master Finn, for insisting we stay on track.'

Finn stared at his second token, and then looked up at the Captain.

'Is that the Crystal Obelisk?' he said, running his fingers over the engraved image.

'It is indeed. Fos Odigos,' Captain M replied.

'Guiding Light,' said Finn, reading the inscription.

The Captain nodded and drew in a deep breath of fresh, cool air.

'Now, let's all focus on the obelisk,' he said.

Shifting his eyes upwards, he tilted his head slightly backwards, and uttered something towards the clouds around them. A low humming sound started vibrating gently behind his voice.

With his hands, he made a sweeping motion above his head and brought them together into a clasp, in front of his chest. Within seconds, sizzling shafts of light started to radiate from the cracks in between the Captain's fingers. He took a step back, and slowly opened both hands.

Cradled in his palms, was a small, glimmering orb of light. At first, it was the size of a golf ball, but as he mumbled his ancient spell, it slowly grew larger until it was almost fist sized.

'Fos odigos,' he said, raising his arms upwards and wiggling his fingers.

He repeated the words a few times and then tossed the orb into the air. It hovered directly in front of his face for a few brief moments, then started to glow brighter and brighter until there was a sphere of white light covering them all.

'Fotise to dromo mas,' said the Captain, asking the orb to shed light on their path.

The air around the orb rippled as it took on a pulsing life

of its own. Seconds later, it released a deafening whooshing sound, and like a shooting star, launched in the direction of the Crystal Obelisk.

'Look at it goooo,' said Finn.

The orb smashed into the Obelisk and wrapped it in a sphere of crackling silver light.

Whoaaa - ahhh - wow!' they all gasped out loud.

A split second later, an almighty gush of wind howled across the whole island. It surged towards the explorers, bringing with it a swirling mass of wet leaves and dust, nearly sweeping them off their feet.

Not long after, the wind died down and the thick fog began to slowly disperse, replaced by a very thin veil of light mist. The Crystal Obelisk was now shining clear and bright.

And so, the explorers followed the path on the left and swiftly climbed upwards towards the beacon of light, in the direction of the Diavolo Drop.

10

AORATOS MAGNITIS
*
INVISIBLE MAGNET

Winding steeply upwards, the path clung to the side of the dark grey anti-Avaton Tower. The ground was a slippery mess in many places, and everyone had to jump over endless puddles to stay dry. The sun's rays tried hard to break through, but it was still misty and pretty damp.

'Come on,' encouraged the Captain, trying to keep the pace up.

By his calculations, it would take anything up to three hours of steady walking to get to the Crystal Obelisk. Climbing in single file, the group stayed as close as possible to the solid rock face. To the left there was a thin line of vegetation, the only thing protecting them from a terrifying drop below. No one dared lean towards it, not even to steal a quick glance.

A relentless calf-burning climb through a series of never-ending zigzags went on and on for what seemed like miles. The last remnants of the unnatural mist were slowly driven away by the sun, and soon its light was blazing out of a very clear sky.

'Have we got any water left?' Holly asked the Captain.

'My mouth is so dry,' said Jack, sticking out his tongue.

'Same here,' said Finn.

'Any moment now,' said the Captain.

Soon after he spoke, the path opened up into a wider, shady pocket of lush green. Trees like weeping willows draped down on either side of the path and to their right, water sprang from the mouth of a statue of a bull's head, that had been carved into the rock.

'H2O,' said Akira.

Jack rushed straight to the spring and started gulping the cold water noisily and fast. His breathing soon became difficult, forcing him to throw his head back and gasp for air. Five seconds later he let off another one of his loud, fruity belches.

'*Woo – wee*, that was a cracker,' said Finn.

'Gross! Didn't your mother teach you to cover your mouth and say excuse me?' Akira scolded him.

Jack smiled sheepishly and shrugged his shoulders as if to say 'sorry'. With a long sigh of satisfaction, he collapsed on the ground with his arms and legs spread-eagled. When everyone had taken it in turns to drink, they flopped down, and for a while, just listened to the soothing sound of rushing water.

The world seemed very calm up here. After their trials and tribulations along Power Coast and in the Monster Caves, there was now a sense that they had crossed into a special place, far removed from turmoil and challenges.

This moment of tranquillity was the perfect time to introduce the next Life Secret.

'Does anyone know where their RAS is?' said the Captain, with a very serious expression on his face.

They all looked up, stunned.

'I beg your pardon,' Akira said, her eyes open wide.

At first the Captain grimaced, trying to smother his laugh, but soon threw his head back and burst into gales of laughter.

'Not your ass, Akira,' he said.

His voice was spiced with chuckles, and nobody had a clue as to what the Captain was going on about.

'I think he's lost his marbles,' muttered Finn out of the corner of his mouth.

'*Shhh*, he might hear,' whispered Holly.

'No, no, no - I mean, your RAS,' said the Captain, spelling the letters out, one by one.

'Sounds the same to me,' said Akira, wondering if this was some kind of joke.

'Your Reticular Activating System,' said the Captain, enunciating every word very distinctly. 'Pretty impressive words, eh?'

'*Ohhh*,' said Holly, as if she understood.

But then let out a giggle and said,

'Still sounds the same to me.'

'Or more like an icky disease,' said Jack, with a smirk.

The Captain shook his head and then made himself comfortable on a flat stone slab, as he began his explanation about a system that would help the GeeBees in the achievement of their goals.

'Your RAS,' he said pulling a funny face, 'is a bundle of nerves that sits in the lower back of the brain. It's about the size of your little finger.'

'That's a really long name for something so little,' Isabelle remarked.

'Well, it may be small in size, but it has a very important role,' responded Captain M. 'It's the portal through which nearly all information from our senses enters the brain.'

'You mean … our sight and hearing,' said Akira.

The Captain nodded.

'And skin,' added Finn, straight away. 'I mean touch.'

'What about smell, and taste?' said Isabelle.

'Yes, your five senses,' responded the Captain. 'Your RAS acts like a sophisticated filter system, allowing certain information into the brain, and leaving the rest out.'

'Why do we need a filter?' asked Akira.

'Well, there's no way that the brain can pay attention to all of the information that it receives from these five sensory organs,' said the Captain. 'It would go into overload if it did … and you'd go potty!'

'How much information are we talking about?' asked Jack.

'Millions of bits of information every second, about everything that's going on in the world around you.'

'Millions! Really?' said Finn.

'That's impossible,' said Akira.

'And yet, it is effiktable Akira,' said the Captain.

To help the GeeBees get a better idea about what he was talking about, he asked them to think about the sense of hearing.

'Take twenty seconds - listen to every sound going on around you at the moment.'

And so, they all remained completely silent for a while, listening intently.

'I can hear the breeze,' said Akira.

'Yes, what else?'

'The running water,' said Isabelle.

'My breathing,' said Holly.

'I can even hear my heartbeat,' Isabelle said, sitting

up excitedly.

'Jack's disgusting belch,' said Akira.

They all burst into fits of laughter.

'Everybody's laughter,' Finn said a second later.

'What about the birds?' said Isabelle.

'Yes, all of those, and many, many more subtle sounds in the background,' said the Captain.

Sounds that were going on all around them, but that no one had noticed before, because they were all so focussed on what the Captain was saying.

'Now, this doesn't just apply to sound. It happens with all the senses.'

'Even with touch?' asked Isabelle.

'Absolutely, Izzy,' the Captain said. 'In fact, our skin is roughly twenty square feet, with a million nerve cells that detect pressure, pain and temperature all at once.'

'*Whoa*, that's incredible,' said Isabelle, examining her hands.

'So, you mean we're sensing loads of things every moment without even realising?' said Akira.

'Exactly,' replied the Captain.

'What about our sight?' asked Jack

The Captain's eyes gleamed at the thought of sharing yet another little scientific titbit.

'The human eye captures more than 300 megapixels of visual information every second.'

'What, even better than even my camera?' Jack said.

'So, we see a lot more than we think we see as well,' Akira said.

The Captain nodded.

'Our senses are constantly bombarding our brain with information. And this is where your RAS kicks in.'

The explorers chuckled nervously under their breath at the sound of the word RAS

'Yourass, yourass, yourass,' repeated Holly, biting the inside of her lip to keep her from laughing out loud.

'Your big ass,' laughed Jack aloud.

The Captain folded his arms over his chest and pretended to look unimpressed. He cleared his throat and continued his explanation.

'Think of your RAS as a gatekeeper that works for your brain,' he said. 'It selects the information that is most relevant for your conscious mind to pay attention to.'

'You mean important information,' said Akira.

'Yes, that's right,' answered the Captain.

'So …' Isabelle said pausing, 'how does the RAS know what's important and what isn't?'

'By what you focus on the most,' replied the Captain.

'What do you mean?' asked Holly.

'Well, there's certain types of information that always get through the gates of the RAS. For example - the sound of your name being called.'

The Captain called out Jack's name.

'Yes,' replied Jack, automatically lifting his head up.

'You see,' said the Captain, smiling at Jack. 'Your name is something important to you, so it got through your gatekeeper.'

'Point taken, Captain,' said Jack, giving him a salute.

'That's so strange,' said Finn, recalling something that had happened to him in the past.

He'd been given a black HOY Bonaly 26" disc bike for his birthday earlier that year.

'I'd never seen one like it before. It's got really chunky tyres. After I got it and went out riding on it for the first time, I saw two more, exactly the same. I swear I'd never seen them before,' said Finn.

'Yes, Finn. That's exactly the example I was looking for,' said the Captain. 'You see, the other bikes were always there, but you just didn't notice them because they weren't on your RAS radar.'

'That is awesome,' said Finn.

'But there's more to the RAS radar than just picking up on things that are of interest or relevant to us,' the Captain continued. 'The RAS also plays a very important role when you are setting a goal for yourself.'

'Howz that?' said Jack.

'Well, when you set a goal that you really want, it's something that is always on your mind. In other words, by setting a clear goal, you're letting your RAS know that anything associated with that goal is important to you.'

'Okay, and so …' said Akira.

'By focussing on something that you really want - in other words something you have a strong positive feeling about - then your RAS will bring to your attention anything associated with that thing,' continued the Captain.

'Which means …' Akira said, impatiently.

'You then become like an invisible magnet,' said the Captain, 'drawing towards you all the things that will help you in the achievement of your goal.'

'So, what you're saying is that our RAS is working, whether we have set it on purpose or not,' said Akira.

'Exactly! So, doesn't it make sense then to set some goals, and programme your RAS to pay attention to things you care about?' said the Captain.

'Rather than spending time thinking about what we don't

want, or are afraid of,' said Isabelle.

She immediately thought of all the negative thoughts and beliefs she had had in the past about what she couldn't be or achieve.

The Captain nodded enthusiastically.

'You see, what we want to do is make the vision of tomorrow, stronger than the memory of yesterday.'

'Sort of, like, shifting our focus,' said Isabelle.

'Yes Izzy. Make the thoughts of all that we want to be, do and have, stronger than any negative thoughts that may be holding us back from achieving our goals,' said the Captain.

'Can - can't,' said Isabelle, moving her hands up and down as if they were cups of a hanging scale.

'When we set a clear intention, which, in turn gives us a good feeling, we're actually letting out RAS know what to focus on,' said the Captain.

'And then we become invisible magnets,' said Holly, cheerily.

'You've got it,' said the Captain.

There was silence for a moment, as the Gee Bees contemplated what this could mean to them.

'That is the best secret by far,' said Finn, jumping from the ground. 'What are we waiting for then?'

Like released springs, Akira, Jack, Holly and Isabelle immediately stood up, ready for action.

'Here we come,' called out the Captain, his voice echoing like a bass drum.

From where they were all standing, the explorers didn't have a full view of the Obelisk itself; only its light emanating from just around the Diavolo bend.

'It looks like sunrise, just before the sun comes up,' said Finn.

'Yeah, you know it's there, but you can't see it,' Isabelle added.

'I can't wait,' said Holly, clasping her hands together.

And so, they all set off once again until they reached the Diavolo Drop; a sixty-foot curved precipice running along the side of the anti-Avaton Tower. It resembled a bookcase shelf, and seemed barely wide enough for a single person to pass.

A support system was already in place for the crossing, with permanent bolts and anchors built into the rock face. Two rows of parallel ropes were fed tightly through the anchors, acting as a handrail.

Captain M walked towards a tall, deep opening in the rock face.

'I'm just going to get the harnesses,' he said.

Turning his body sideways he squeezed through the huge crack in the rock and disappeared.

'How did he fit in there?' Finn said, peeking into the opening.

'It's like the tower's swallowed him whole,' said Jack.

A hand suddenly darted out of the crack causing everyone to jump with fright.

'*Aggh*, what the …' said Finn.

He tumbled backwards and fell to the ground with a thud. Jack burst out laughing at the hilarious way that Finn fell.

The Captain squeezed himself back out of the opening, armed with a pile of simple rope-chest harnesses. Brushing the equipment with his hands, he cleaned the dust and cobwebs off and dropped them onto the ground.

'Right, let's get these on,' he said.

He wriggled into the largest harness, which was simple enough to put on. A few moments later, they were all ready for the crossing.

'What's this for?' asked Jack, holding a dangling metal object.

'It's a quick release hook,' said the Captain.

As a safety measure, they would each attach their hook to the safety line, running waist-high all the way along the crossing. Akira heaved a sigh of relief knowing she wouldn't have to worry about falling, even if she slipped.

'We're going to do this nice and easy,' said the Captain, giving everyone's harness a final check.

He talked them through what was always the most terrifying part of the crossing; stepping onto the ledge. After a lengthy discussion of the "dos" and "don'ts" the Captain asked,

'So, who wants to take the lead?'

'I will,' was Finn's spontaneous answer.

Finn had spent many a summer break canyoneering and tackling mountain passages with his uncle, proving himself to be both practical and capable.

The rest of the group watched on in anticipation, as Finn hooked himself to the railing and placed one foot on the ledge. He slowly put his full weight on it to test its strength. Then, easing his other foot alongside it, he slid his leading foot forward once more.

'Everything's okay,' he said, glancing back at everyone.

'Lead the way then, Master Finn,' said the Captain.

He gave one of his big, beaming smiles and Finn couldn't do anything but smile back. Slowly but surely, he crossed to the other side using the fixed ropes and creeping shrubs that covered the rock wall as good hold for his hands.

Isabelle went next, followed by Jack and Holly. One by one, they edged along the ledge, pressing their bodies close against the rocky side of the mountain.

When it was Akira's turn to make a move, she took a great

lungful of air, and hooked herself onto the secure rope railing.

'That's too narrow,' she thought, staring at the ledge.

The rock looked deeply weathered and weak, almost ready to crumble under the slightest pressure.

'I can't do this,' she whimpered to the Captain.

'Take some deep breaths through your nose,' he said, in a calming voice.

He told her to focus on what she wanted rather than on what she feared.

'Come on Akira, you can do it,' called out Holly from the other side.

'It's much easier than it looks,' added Jack.

'It's impossible,' said Akira, firmly holding onto the railing with her hands

'Only if you believe it is,' said the Captain, serenely.

Isabelle's voice called out loudly, 'It's effiktable!'

At that moment, Akira's stubborn streak came to life. If everyone else had managed the crossing, she thought to herself, then so could she. Her feet were hesitant at first but after a few initial whimpering sounds, Akira took her first baby steps. Afraid to trust the full weight of her body to her harness, she ended up gripping the rope a lot tighter than she needed to.

'*Mmmm*,' she groaned, shutting her lips tight together to stop herself from saying anything.

She was still scared, but made herself concentrate on everything the Captain had told her.

'Focus on your goal,' he said gently.

And so, Akira kept her gaze firmly locked on the glow emanating from Obelisk and began to move. Everything was going well until around the middle of the bend, when she had a sudden urge to look down into the abyss below. She felt like she was about to fall and clutched the railing so tightly, that her knuckles turned almost white.

'One wrong move,' Akira thought to herself, her body completely tensing up.

She became frozen to the spot, her jaws clenched, and her heart pounded uncontrollably.

'Just focus on where you're going, Akira, and everything will be fine,' said the Captain, from just behind her.

He took hold of Akira's sweaty hand and reminded her that her harness was locked onto the railing. No matter what happened, she was safe.

'Just breeeaath - long and deep.'

When she did so, Akira found her body slowly beginning to relax and soon enough, she started moving with greater ease.

'Come on, have a look over here,' Finn called out, beckoning her with his hand.

'You'll never guess what we just saw,' said Holly.

Knowing that her ordeal was almost over and with only a few more steps to go, Akira unwound even more. She also sensed an inexplicable, pulling sensation, as if she was being drawn towards something.

'Can you feel that?' she asked the Captain, turning her head back to him ever so slightly.

'The more open you are to possibility, the more your invisible magnet works its magic,' said the Captain, nodding in a reassuring gesture.

The ledge soon widened, turning into a trail that led away from the edge. Akira unclipped her hook, her legs still wobbling a bit. From this safe distance, she peered down at the purple plains, green forests and magnificent sea views, thankful that her ordeal was over.

'Token number eight belongs to you I believe,' said the Captain.

He handed Akira the Invisible Magnet token, with the words Aoratos Magnitis engraved around the outer edge. She rubbed her thumb against the image and said, 'Invisible magnet.'

'You have the power inside of you that you need, in order to bring all the things that will help you in the achievement of your goals,' the Captain told her.

Akira stared at the token momentarily, and then looked at the Captain intently. Her expression held a silent thank you for standing by her side.

'Come quickly,' called out Isabelle, as she turned the corner, quickening her pace slightly.

'I've never seen anything quite like it,' said Holly.

11

MIKRA DORA
*
SMALL GIFTS

A little further on, the trail led them through a narrow pass and into an old stone quarry. Standing dramatically in the centre, was a massive crystal obelisk, rising at least thirty feet into the sky. Like a giant diamond that had been struck by the sun, it radiated its pure white light, and pulsed with a life of its own.

Finn ran over to the Obelisk and stood under it. He looked tiny and insignificant in comparison to the towering pillar.

'This is humungous,' he said. 'How could something so tall and straight rise up from this flat piece of land?'

'Is it a totem pole?' asked Holly, trying to make sense of the carvings that covered its surface.

'It looks more like some kind of shrine,' said Akira.

'Yeah,' said Jack, rubbing his hands. 'Maybe for human sacrifices.'

'Jaaaack! Shut up,' said Holly.

'This, my friends, is made of crystal quartz,' said the Captain, stroking the glistening obelisk.

He explained how since the beginning of time, the people of Aydagar believed strongly that the natural world held supernatural powers. They believed in gods that ruled over the valleys, mountains, rivers and trees of the island.

'This crystal was considered to be eternal ice from the heavens; water that has been frozen so deeply, that it would always remain solid.'

'It's cloudy, but almost see-through,' said Holly, touching the surface.

'What's that up there?' asked Isabelle, pointing to an engraving that stood out from the surface of the stone.

It was a circle, with nine triangular rays beaming outwards in all directions.

'That is the Star of Argead, the royal symbol of Aydagar,' said the Captain.

'Wait a minute,' said Isabelle.

Without another word, she walked up to the Captain and held his left hand up.

'The ring,' she said.

On the Captain's forefinger was a gold signet ring, with the exact same symbol engraved into the flat top. He had been wearing it the whole time, but up until this moment, no-one had noticed.

'What does it all mean?' asked Holly.

'There is much to learn about the powers of crystals,' said the Captain, 'but you will learn all about that next time.'

'Next time?' said Isabelle, turning round sharply with a startled look on her face.

'You mean ...' said Holly, pausing for a response from their guide.

The Captain simply gave one of his usual nods but didn't give them an answer. More pressing for the moment, was the fact that night was drawing in. The horizon around them was starting to fill with the colours of sunset; swirling shades of orangey-red and flushed delicate pinks.

The group had to move quickly if they wanted to arrive at their destination before dark. So, they crossed over the stone, arch bridge that joined the two towers, and walked upwards for a little while longer; until the path came to an abrupt end. With no access by foot from here onwards, the only way for them to reach the summit, was straight up the vertical rock face.

'But if there's no road, how did the temple get up there?' said Jack looking upwards.

'It did so, only after many, many years of effort,' said the Captain.

'But how?' asked Jack.

In answer to his question, Captain M related the most incredible story about three hermit monks, whose names were Arathos, Andronicus and Athanasios.

'They were the first humans to climb these soaring vertical towers, seven hundred years ago. They settled in the caves and hollows, near the summit of the Avaton Tower.'

'Why would they want to live here in the middle of nowhere?' asked Akira.

'Because they wanted to be closer to their gods,' said the Captain.

'Rather them than me,' she muttered in response.

With no steps and little access to the rest of the island, the hermits lived their lives in isolation and solitude. Their only contact with the world below was by sitting in a basket or net hitched over a hook, which they would hoist up and down by means of a rope.

'It was the perfect place for them to achieve absolute isolation, and to discover internal peace and harmony,' said the Captain.

He described in colourful detail, how the monks would rise before sunrise to pray and meditate, developing skills of the mind and body that most other people could never dream of.

Between the three of them, the wise men recorded the words that their gods had spoken, on hundreds of scrolls, in golden ink; thousands of prayers, spells and teachings that held the secret to living a life of true happiness, love and abundance.

'One night, the monks each had the same powerful dream,' said the Captain.

'What dream?' whispered Isabelle.

'The supreme god, Azef, appeared to them, asking them to build a temple. A temple so magnificent, so beautiful that it would have no equal in the land. It took many, many years to build it.'

'What, just the three of them?' said Jack.

'On their own?' Finn said.

'Not on their own,' replied the Captain. 'Tribes from all over the land of Aydagar came to help.'

Using ropes, nets and ladders, everything from people, supplies and building materials was suspended in baskets and pulled to the top.

'They chose to undertake this task not because it was easy, but because it was hard. In fact, almost impossible.'

But they succeeded in this great achievement, through the driving force of their faith, and a clear vision of what the finished temple would look like.

'What happened to the scrolls?' asked Akira.

'They were taken to Golden Chamber, inside the Avaton Temple,' the Captain replied.

'Golden Chamber?' gasped Holly, clasping her hands to her chest dramatically.

'What else is up there?' Isabelle asked.

'All will be revealed in good time,' Captain M said, his green eyes flickering in the light of the crystal.

Up until now, a clear view of the temple had not been possible. Most of the time, the Avaton peaks were shrouded in rolling mists, so any onlooker was only able to catch a few glimpses every now and then.

'How will we get up there?' Akira asked.

She knew the answer, but hoped she was wrong.

'Suspended in that, like in the good ol' days,' replied the Captain.

He walked over to a large woven wicker basket, that looked like something that would be under a hot air balloon.

'Oh, no,' said Akira, letting out a heavy sigh.

'How many of us can fit in here?' asked Holly, already standing by the basket.

'Two at a time,' said the Captain, opening the basket door.

'And who's going to pull us up?' asked Finn.

'He is,' said the Captain, waving at a jolly face peeking from over the summit.

Philoxenias was one of seven monks who now lived in the temple area. Dressed in brown robes, he was a little bald on the top, had a round face and chubby cheeks.

'Philoxenias - doesn't that mean something to do with a friend?' said Akira, quickly snapping out of her worrisome thoughts.

'A friend to all strangers,' the Captain said, nodding.

Now, Philoxenias had the important task of making his guests feel at home, offering them hospitality, food and drink. The maintenance of livestock, vegetable gardens and vineyards, as well as the special duty of looking after the scrolls, were left to the other six monks living here.

Akira looked at the ropes that connected to the pulley system. Although they were clearly thick enough to hold the basket, they nevertheless looked a little too weathered for her liking.

'How often do they replace the ropes?' she said, like a survey inspector.

'Whenever they break,' answered Captain M.

Akira's mouth hung open, and a split second later, the Captain let out a loud, raucous laugh that could be heard in the valley below. He couldn't help himself, and for a short while roared with laughter, until his face turned beet red.

'Just kidding,' he said, wiping the tears running down his cheeks.

'Good one,' said Jack, giving a thumbs up.

He jumped into the basket with Holly. The ropes automatically tightened, as Philoxenias started pulling and tugging with all his strength. A few jerks later, the basket slowly rose into the air, swaying as it inched upwards.

'Hang on tight,' said Holly.

She held onto the edge of the basket and spread her feet a little wider to steady herself. It was the only way she could keep her balance.

For several minutes, the ropes above them groaned as they stretched, the pulleys creaking noisily under the strain. Philoxenias kept up a steady pull-pull rhythm, until finally Jack and Holly were transported to the summit.

They were both greeted with a happy smile and words of welcome, from the monk who was not much taller than they were.

'I'm so glad you're here,' said Philoxenias.

'Glad to be here,' said Jack.

He pulled a funny face at the monk's slightly distorted high-pitched voice, which didn't really belong to an adult.

'Thank you,' Holly said, excitedly.

Up and down the basket went two more times, and it wasn't long before the group were once again reunited at the top of the tower.

By now the last of the sun had disappeared and the night was closing in on them. As the beauty of the island below them was being swallowed by darkness, some of the monks set about lighting all the fire torches.

'Come with me,' Philoxenias told them.

His upper left eyelid twitched rapidly as if he was getting a small electric shock.

'Is he winking at us?' said Jack, trying to keep a straight face.

'*Shhh*, be quiet, he'll hear you,' Akira said in a hoarse whisper.

She jabbed her elbow into his ribs.

Philoxenias smiled a broad, nearly toothless grin and beckoned them forward. Staying only a few steps behind, Captain M and the GeeBees followed the monk along the tall perimeter wall, that snaked around the upper edge of the Avaton Tower. As the group came around a bend, two massive, wooden gates came into view.

It took all of Philoxenias' strength to push one of the heavy wooden gates open. Isabelle was the first to walk a few steps into the courtyard, and what she saw took her breath away.

'*Whoaaaa!*' said Isabelle, catching her breath for a few

seconds and then exhaling slowly.

It was how she imagined heaven would look, as you stepped through the Pearly Gates. Burning torches ran along the outer walls of the temple courtyard and throughout the flowering gardens. Together with the glimmering moon in the night sky, there was just enough light for them to see their surroundings.

'Are we in Paradise?' asked Holly, in a low whisper.

She moved closer to Isabelle and reached out for her hand, staring in awe at the tall, white building at the end of the stone path.

Rising high in front of them was Avaton Temple, a place where few had trodden. Made of milky quartz, it resembled a temple from the times of the ancient Greeks. A single row of columns ran around the temple, four along the front of a porch area, and eight down each side.

Inside the columns, was a chamber made of four rectangular solid walls with no windows, not even a door. A flight of seven deep steps running the whole width of the temple, led up to the entrance.

The GeeBees stood in silence for a few moments, until Philoxenias finally spoke.

'Are you hungry?' he asked them.

He quirked an eyebrow and shot them a lopsided toothless grin. Turning back around, he promptly walked away from them, his footsteps echoing on the stone floor of the courtyard.

'I, for one am starving,' said Finn.

He immediately took off after the strange little fellow.

'Let's order pizza?' said Jack called from behind him.

'Well, if its pizza, you're paying,' replied Finn, looking back at his friend but still walking.

'Two pizzas coming up,' said Jack, pretending to write down

169

the order.

'Naaa ...' said Holly. 'It'll take too long to get up here.'

'You're so silly,' Akira said, shaking her head.

Philoxenias guided his guests off the main path, across an area of lush ferns and exotic flowers; towards a gazebo, covered with dainty, white climbing roses that smelt of the most exquisite perfume. They all sat down around a circular table laden with jugs of water, various bread rolls and fresh fruits.

While everyone ate busily and chattered, Isabelle munched on a pear. She wasn't really interested in food. She wanted answers and was far more intrigued by all that awaited them in the temple.

Isabelle also felt a tinge of sadness about what lay beyond that; for she knew that her adventure on Aydagar, would soon be over.

'Captain M,' she started to say.

Her throat tightened as she tried to say the words but couldn't finish her sentence.

Captain M saw in Isabelle's eyes what she was thinking.

'This is just the beginning Izzy, not the end,' he said.

'What do you mean?' asked Akira.

Akira may have been eating, but always had her ears alert to everything going on around her.

Captain M addressed them all, telling them that they were in the early days of their life's journey. A journey of self-discovery, of finding out who they truly were and what they were capable of. A journey that, so far, had shown them that with the right mindset and a deep desire, anything was possible.

'Anything is effiktable,' said Holly and Isabelle at the same time.

170

They smiled, immediately hooking their little fingers in making a wish.

'If you want it badly enough,' added Finn.

The Captain smiled and nodded.

'As you will find out when you leave Aydagar, and again, when you return,' said the Captain with great gusto.

'So, we are coming back?' said Isabelle.

Her heart almost skipped a beat.

'When? I mean how?' asked Holly.

'Once you incorporate the nine Life Secrets into your lives, you may then return, and discover many other ways to make your dreams come true,' said the Captain.

It was now clear that their first grand adventure on Aydagar, was just a stepping-stone to future explorations.

'Can we all come back?' asked Jack.

The Captain ruffled Jack's thick hair with affection.

'If you practise your Life Secrets, then your return is inevitable.'

Jack grinned with sheepish laughter, feeling a strange sense of relief.

'Now, before we move on,' said the Captain, 'tell me some of the ways you can keep a positive attitude.'

'Laugh - be funny and find humour in any situation,' responded Jack.

'Definitely, Jack,' the Captain said, smiling. 'Laughter is one of my favourite magic potions.'

He stuck out his hand, thumb up, as if counting off on his fingers, and raised his eyebrow questioningly.

'What else?' he said, opening up a second finger.

'Shift your focus, from negative to positive self-talk,' answered Isabelle.

'Yes, Izzy. Our thoughts influence our feelings and then our …' the Captain said, pausing.

'Our behaviour,' said Akira.

The Captain nodded.

'Heart Thoughts,' said Holly, the words flying out of her mouth.

She pulled out of her pocket the token that she had received on the Power Coast.

'Always remember to place your attention on all that is good in you, the person next to you and any situation you are in,' the Captain reminded them.

He continued the tempo of ticking off the points on his fingers.

'What about turning failures into lessons,' said Jack.

'That's right, Jack,' confirmed the Captain. 'There's no such thing as failure - just lessons learnt.'

'Happy friends,' said Holly, pulling on Akira and Isabelle's arms.

'Absolutely, Holly. It's difficult to stay positive when you are surrounded by complainers,' said the Captain, winking at her.

Their guide then leant forward on his forearms and shifted from the right to the left hand, in ticking off his fingers. He told the GeeBees about yet another powerful way to keep a positive mindset.

'Find things to be grateful for,' he said. 'There are always blessings and miracles around us, that we often ignore or take for granted.'

He paused and looked at each one of them in turn.

'When was the last time you were thankful for something,' he asked Holly.

'I've never really thought about it,' she replied. 'But I always say thank you when I'm supposed to.'

'*Ahhh*, but saying thank you is so much more than just being polite, or showing good manners. You can feel gratitude all of the time, even for the smallest of things. Being thankful is a key that opens the door to instant happiness and contentment.'

He made a sound by clicking his middle fingers against his thumb.

'Just think for a moment about all the things that are already yours, that you could be grateful for. Even if things might not be as you would ideally like them to be.'

A minute passed in silence before Isabelle spoke.

'Well, I for one am thankful for my eyesight,' she said. 'My cousin Maggie isn't so lucky.'

Learning that Isabelle's cousin had lost her eyesight, made everyone think long and hard about all the blessings they had in their lives. It wasn't long before the words came rolling out of everyone's mouths.

They were thankful for the life in their bodies, for the air in their lungs and for their limbs. They were thankful for the food on the table and their comfortable beds to sleep in at night. Many others were not in such fortunate positions.

'What about the people that love us?' asked Finn.

'Yes,' said the Captain, nodding. 'And what about the difference you make in other people's lives, and the other way round?'

He also asked them to think about their different character strengths.

'Think about your honesty, perseverance, curiosity, patience and courage in different situations,' he said.

'I never thought about it like that before,' said Jack.

'It's just part of us,' said Akira.

'Yes, part of you that you can be grateful for,' said the Captain.

He asked them to think about what qualities they liked about their friends.

'I like Jack's humour - most of the time,' said Finn.

'Yeah, Jack, you are funny,' said Holly.

Akira also admitted that, although she did find Jack most annoying, and his comments a little simple-minded, she appreciated the fact that he now had a positive intention behind his humour. It was no longer just about putting someone down. Jack smiled to himself when he understood how appreciated he was by his friends.

As a group, they acknowledged the ways they had all benefitted from each other's personality traits; Akira's directness and perseverance, Holly's enthusiasm and playfulness, Isabelle's kindness and resilience and Finn's inquisitiveness and courageous spirit.

'When we express our gratitude for something, it's like we're immediately transported to a good place' said the Captain.

'Yes, it really is that way,' said Akira.

'Some people call it having an attitude of gratitude,' said Captain M.

'I understand what you're saying, but it's not always easy to feel grateful,' said Isabelle.

'I know it isn't,' said the Captain. 'But if you make it a habit to focus on appreciating someone or something, then it will definitely help you have a more positive outlook.'

'And that'll help us get through the more difficult times,' said Holly, cheerfully.

'And give our RAS something to aim for,' said Akira.

The Captain nodded and smiled.

'Is that it then, the ninth secret?' said Finn.

'Indeed, it is,' answered the Captain.

He took the last remaining token out of his pouch and gave it to Isabelle. The simple present that was engraved on it, was a symbol for gratitude.

'The infinite loop stands for everlasting appreciation,' the Captain told her.

'For even the little things in life,' responded Isabelle.

She read out loud the Hellenic words, Mikra Dora, meaning small gifts.

A gust of wind suddenly rushed past them, startling them all. Seemingly out of nowhere, it was so strong it made the torch flames flicker erratically in all directions. The expression on the Captain's face, said clearly that he had sensed something else. He took only a short moment before speaking again.

'The time has come,' he said.

He stood up and turned in the direction of the temple. His eyes went wide for a second and then, he smiled an enormous smile. The explorers stood up at once and as they followed his gaze, saw a tall human-shaped figure, standing between the central columns of the temple porch area. Surrounded by a halo of light, it stood quite still.

'What's that?' Holly asked in a hushed voice.

'It wasn't there when we arrived,' Jack said, quietly but emphatically.

Once again, their questions remained unanswered, as Captain M set off down the central walkway towards the temple.

12

SECRET COMBINATION

The explorers took off after him like a rocket, taking care not to bump into the burning torches either side of the path. As they moved closer towards the temple, the figure on the porch took a few steps forward out of the glowing light.

It turned out to be a striking lady, with luminous blue eyes, soft creamy skin and luxurious snow-white hair that draped down over her shoulders. On her head she wore a cap of lace, and a transparent veil hung from her shoulders over her long, white flowing robes.

'Is she an angel?' said Akira, quietly.

'Oh my gosh,' said Holly, with a sigh.

'She's beautiful,' gasped Isabelle.

Captain M stopped a few feet from the steps, bowed his head and opened his arms wide.

'Haire sofi Aenais,' he called out.

The Captain's voice boomed, echoing as if he was speaking through a loudspeaker. His words of greeting were directed at Aenais, the eternal high priestess of the Avaton Temple.

'Haire kai se sena Mentora, kalos irthate.'

The high priestess greeted the Captain and welcomed everyone; her voice so soft that it barely whispered in their ears. Aenais turned towards the explorers and looked them square in the face, one by one.

'Are you the Great Budding Explorers.'

She raised an enquiring eyebrow and her bright, sparkling blue eyes lit up her whole face.

There was no hesitation and they all answered 'yes'. Truth be known, the GeeBees didn't have the slightest clue whether they were the 'great ones', but after extraordinary adventures on Aydagar, they certainly felt like true Budding Explorers.

Aenais turned to the Captain.

'Are they ready to gain access to the wisdom within the temple?'

'Indeed, they are,' said the Captain.

Tears of joy welled up in his eyes. The tears of a man who had had the honour of being the guide to five, fine explorers.

'Behold the door to the Golden Chamber,' said Aenais, slowly standing to one side.

She opened her arm to her right, showing them the blank, solid wall.

'I can't see a door,' said Finn.

He tilted his head to one side and then the other, looking for something to suggest that there was some kind of entrance there.

'Neither can I,' said Akira.

'Is she kidding?' Jack whispered.

'*Shhh*, maybe it's a secret door,' said Isabelle.

'Wait and see,' said the Captain.

By now, the full moon had marched slowly over their heads

and commenced its descent behind them. As it gradually lowered itself in the sky, the moon began shedding its light onto the façade of the crystal chamber in front of them.

Where the light touched the wall, faint lines gradually started appearing, like fine, hairline cracks running through a stone. As the moon sank lower and lower, its light soon covered the whole of the front wall, revealing an unrecognizable jumble of lines, markings and intricate curvatures.

Then, as if by some magical force, the lines started growing thicker and brighter until finally, forms took shape and the seemingly solid wall was transformed into a large doorway.

'*Whoa*, it IS a door,' said Isabelle.

'How did that happen?' said Finn.

'Now, that's what I call magic,' said Jack, smiling.

The outline of the door glistened in the moonlight and for a while, the GeeBees remained quiet, suspended in surprise. Aenais told them that they had one final challenge to overcome; the opening of the door into the inner chamber.

'To access the inner chamber, you must find the secret combination to this door,' she said. 'Speed is of the essence, there is much to be done before the rising of the morning sun.'

Above the stone door was a semi-circular arch, etched with a series of well-cut and distinctly written words.

'Hrisi Ethousa Epithimion,' said Isabelle, reading out loud the interlaced, gold letters.

'Golden …' said Akira, beginning to translate the words.

She paused, looking towards their guide.

'It's the Golden Chamber of Wishes,' said the Captain.

'What is that exactly?' asked Isabelle.

'Maybe there's a genie in there,' said Finn.

'Or maybe we'll find a magic lamp,' giggled Holly.

Endless scenarios rolled through their minds, each one more exciting than the other.

'But there's no doorknob, so how can we open it?' said Jack.

'Not another door!' said Akira.

'Maybe it can only be opened from the inside,' said Finn.

'That doesn't make sense,' said Jack.

He walked up to the door and pressed both his palms flat against it.

'How about if you push,' said Holly.

Jack used his shoulder to shove hard, but nothing happened. Finn and Holly laid their backs against the door and crouched a little, digging their heels into the ground.

'One, two, three,' Finn counted as the three of them gave a huge, almighty push.

They huffed and they puffed, but try as they might, it still wouldn't budge. Not even so much as a creak.

'Maybe, we just have to say something,' said Akira.

'What, like open sesame,' said Jack, sarcastically.

'Well, can you think of anything better?'

'Yes, I can actually,' he said. 'Prepare to be amazed.'

Jack turned around to face the door and twiddled his fingers all round it, like a magician.

'Open for meeee,' he said in a deep, theatrical voice.

When nothing happened, they all burst out laughing at Jack's sheer ridiculousness. Akira, who felt she was the most sensible one among them, had already turned her attention to the Hellenic lettering running along the left side of the door.

'That must be a clue,' she said, reading the inscription.

The letters were familiar, but the words were disjointed and made no sense to her at all. Akira turned to the Captain, looking for guidance.

'Can you help?' she said

Captain M nodded his head slightly and began the translation of the single sentence.

'Add the tokens to the Argead rays and watch the door open without delay.'

'Not another riddle,' Jack said.

'It's not a riddle, it's an instruction,' said Akira.

'What rays?' said Finn.

'Think, there must be a logical explanation,' said Akira.

The Captain repeated the words once more.

'Add the tokens to the Argead rays and watch the door open without delay.'

As Isabelle swayed backward and forward on her heels with her hands in her pockets, all of a sudden, it hit her. She took a few steps backwards and her face brightened.

'That's it,' she said, beckoning her friends closer.

'What is it, Izzy?' asked Akira.

'Those are the nine rays,' Isabelle said, pointing to the elongated triangular shapes running around what looked like a sun.

'One, two, three, four, five, six, seven, eight, nine,' said Holly, the triangular rays.

'Of course,' Finn said.

'The nine Life Secrets,' said Holly.

'You're a genius Izzy,' Akira grabbed her friend's hand.

'Yeah Izzy, well spotted,' said Jack.

Covering almost the entire surface of the temple door was an image of the shining Argead Star.

At the end of each sun ray was an inlay the size of a two-penny coin. Nine inlays all in all, with an inscription in Hellenic running from the tip of each ray, along the central axis towards the circular sun.

'See these?' said Jack.

He moved his fingers over the smooth circular indentations, curious to see if they were some form of secret trigger that would open the door.

'They're lined with some kind of metal.'

'Your finger might get stuck,' Holly squeaked.

She reached across and pulled at his sleeve, but she wasn't fast enough.

'Get off me,' Jack snapped.

He pulled free and pressed his finger hard in the inlay. Nothing happened. He pressed another circular indentation but again, nothing happened.

'C'mon, try them all,' said Akira, impatiently breathing down his neck.

Jack spun around and gave her the death glare.

'I was just about to do that,' he said, gritting his teeth.

'Suit yourself,' she told him, folding her arms and taking a step back.

Jack took his time, pressing his finger into all the inlays. Everyone held their breath, waiting for something to happen, but nothing did. Meanwhile, Isabelle was still standing in the background trying to make sense of the pattern on the door. With her hands deep in her pockets, she absentmindedly jiggled the contents with her fingers. It didn't take long before the penny dropped.

'The tokens,' she said.

She pulled out four tokens from her pocket.

'Join the tokens with the Argead rays and watch the door open without delay,' Akira said, clenching her fists and trembling with excitement.

'That's it,' said Holly.

'You're a double genius,' said Akira.

'Yeah, really,' admitted Jack. 'Not even with my infinite powers of observation did I get that'.

Isabelle was now glowing. Being acknowledged and appreciated by her peers was still something quite new to her and she basked in the warm, fuzzy feelings that rushed through her.

'Let's try it,' said Jack, pulling the token from his pocket.

'Hang on,' said Akira, taking on her teacher voice.

She walked up to the Argead and ran her finger along a ray situated on northern part of the sun.

'That's my token,' she said, recalling the Life Secret about the Invisible Magnet.

Reaching into her pocket Akira placed her token in her open palm and checked the writing just to be sure.

'Aoratos Magnitis,' she said, reading the inscription out loud.

'Oh yes,' said Jack, taking his token from his pocket.

He walked to the fifth ray and pushed his Skia sto Nero token into the inlay. But as soon as he moved his hand away, the token fell down to the ground.

'Why did it do that?' he said, baffled.

'There's more to this than meets the eye,' said Akira.

'Maybe we have to start from the beginning,' said Finn.

'It does make sense to start with the first secret,' Isabelle agreed.

'It's worth a try,' said Jack.

'Let's move clockwise starting with the first secret,' said Akira.

And so, they began from the beginning, from when they first arrived at the Power Coast.

'Okay, what were the first three secrets about?' Isabelle said, confidently.

They all took their tokens out of their pockets and examined the inscriptions for a while. It was at the Power Coast that they learnt about the power of their extraordinary minds and why we achieve what we believe.

'The first Life Secret was Kiriarho Mialo,' Isabelle said. 'It was about the conscious and subconscious mind.'

She didn't have to read anything because she remembered off by heart the Hellenic words for Master Brain. Gripping the token between her thumb and forefinger, Isabelle stretched up on tiptoes and leant forward towards the top of the Argead Star. As she positioned the first token just over the first inlay, a strange thing happened.

Isabelle felt an inexplicable suction, as if something was pulling the token from her fingers. She gripped tight but the invisible force was stronger than her. A split second later the token popped out of her fingers and with a soft metallic click sound, slotted into its rightful place.

'Did you see that?' she said. 'It was like some kind of magnet.'

'That was weird,' said Jack.

He tried to remove the token, but it was as tightly sealed as a can of beans. It wouldn't budge no matter how hard he tried to dig it out with his fingernail.

There was a sudden ripple of excitement as the explorers found themselves one step closer to figuring out the combination that would open the door.

'My turn,' said Holly.

The second ray had the words Skepseis Kardias running along its central axis.

'Heart Thoughts,' said Holly, as she remembered the secret

183

about thoughts and beliefs.

There was the same metallic click sound, as the token automatically slotted into place. The system worked, which meant they were on the right track.

'Who had the third token,' asked Akira, taking charge.

'Me,' said Isabelle.

'You again?' said Jack.

'Yep, with Smokey Mirror,' said Isabelle, holding up her token in the air.

It was up at the lake where Isabelle learnt about the power of the words she said to herself and how to shift her focus. She slotted in her token, feeling all goosepimply as she remembered her guardian angel, Aziel.

'I was number four,' said Finn. 'Vale Oria.'

He flipped his token into the air with his thumb, and as it began to fall back down, he caught it in his right hand and flopped it on the back of his left hand.

'Draw the line,' he said, recalling the moment he said a big 'no' to Jack.

'Who's next?' said Akira.

'Finally, my turn,' said Jack.

He placed the Shadow in the Water token in its rightful place, relishing the sound of the click-pop that it made.

'Good riddance to that,' he said, referring to the green Monster of Failure.

'Five down, four to go,' said Holly, rubbing her hands together with excitement.

'We're over half-way through. Who's next?' said Akira.

Isabelle was already one step ahead.

'Winds of Change,' she said, slotting her token into the sixth inlay.

Isabelle's resilience when facing of the Monster of the Unknown had left her feeling so very empowered.

'We got the last three tokens climbing the Towers,' said Finn.

It was during their ascent of the Avaton heights that they had learnt about creating a vision for their lives, and how they could start turning their dreams into reality.

'Number seven, Guiding Light,' said Finn.

He took great delight in holding the token close enough to the inlay and watching it get sucked into place.

'Does everyone remember their RAS?' Akira followed on.

Everyone became quiet and stared at each other, trying to stifle their laugh at the funny sounding word for a very small part of the brain.

'Our Invisible Magnet will help us achieve our goals,' said Akira, placing her token on the last but one ray.

With eight tokens in place, it was now up to Isabelle to complete the Argead Star combination.

'Mikra Dora,' she said.

She approached the ninth ray that pointed true north and placed her Small Gifts token in the inlay.

Silence followed. No one spoke. Nobody dared to speak, but every eye rested on the door. Then there was a sudden grinding sound of stone against stone that continued for several moments.

The GeeBees cringed as the airlocked doors suddenly opened with an eerie creaking sound. What they saw beyond that left them simply wonderstruck.

13

CHAMBER OF WISHES

Aenais stared deep into Isabelle's eyes, took a deep breath and smiled affectionately. Slowly, she moved onto Akira, Jack, Finn and Holly, giving them exactly the same silent communication. No words were exchanged, because none needed to be.

'Before you all enter the Golden Chamber, there is something you must do' she said, in a solemn but kind voice.

'I want you to leave all bad feelings behind you. Feelings such as worry, sadness or even embarrassment; for negative feelings have no place in the Golden Chamber of Wishes.'

Aenais stood there quietly, pausing for a few moments before continuing.

'If you have any such feelings - just imagine that they are autumn leaves being blown far, far away by the wind.'

No sooner had she spoken than a gentle breeze picked up her words and carried them away from the porch, outwards into the dark, velvety skies.

'Have you done that?' she asked.

The GeeBees all nodded in agreement.

The high priestess then spoke to the explorers about love, dreams and abundance. Everyone was captivated by the unusual words of wisdom and understanding that fell from her lips.

'Are you ready to step through?' Aenais asked, holding her hand out towards the inner chamber.

'I guess so,' said Holly, grinning sheepishly.

'There can be no guessing,' Aenais warned.

She repeated her question once more, 'Are you ready to step in?'

'Yes,' replied Holly.

'Ready as we'll ever be,' said Finn, coming sharply to attention.

While this was all going on, the Captain had taken a few steps back and was leaning against a column.

'Aren't you coming with us?' Isabelle asked him.

'I'll be waiting for you here,' he said. 'It's okay, go ahead.'

It was an unexpected reply, but Isabelle shrugged her shoulders and joined the others behind Aenais, as she walked into the temple.

The Golden Chamber was vast and seemed even bigger on the inside than it did on the outside. A colonnade of white, crystal pillars ran along each side, rising up from the gold-speckled mosaic floor. Glittering gold acanthus leaves twined up and around the columns towards a dark ceiling, encrusted with thousands of gems. They twinkled and sparkled like stars in the darkest sky.

Every so often, flaming torches were set in brackets against the wall, giving off a gentle golden light. Most of the light though, came not from the torches, but from a golden glow in the heart of the chamber.

Three steps led from the ground level down to a round, sunken floor area. In the middle of it was an open fireplace where logs were burning. Surrounding that was a circular couch made of milky crystal quartz, covered with colourful royal violet, light gold and turquoise scatter cushions.

The jewel in the crown though, was a cone-shaped transparent chimney breast, which seemed to be floating in the air above the fireplace.

'Make yourselves comfortable,' Aenais told them.

Quickly, the GeeBees settled back against the big fluffy cushions. Everyone except for Finn that is. Curiosity had got the better of him and he bent down so he could look up at the free-floating chimney.

'How can it stay up?'

He stretched himself on tiptoes to examine the top end.

'Where's the smoke going?' said Jack.

'I dunno,' Finn said.

The chimney breast was definitely fixed in place, but it didn't touch the ceiling; nor was it joined to the fireplace below in any way. Stranger still, smoke was being drawn into the chimney breast, but none was coming out of the top end.

'Maybe it's got wings,' Jack sniggered.

'Not funny,' Akira said immediately.

'Things may not always be as they appear,' said Aenais. 'Logic does not explain everything.'

'But …' said Akira.

Before she could finish her sentence, Aenais put her finger to her lips and said '*shhh.*' There may have been many unanswered questions high on Akira's list but as Aenais pointed out, there was a much more important reason for why they were all here.

'We will go on a journey,' she said, pausing to look at them one by one as she did earlier.

'But we've only just got here,' said Jack.

'*Derr*, obviously not that kind of journey,' Akira said.

'*Derr* to you, grouch.'

Jack gave a long sigh, flopped right back on the cushions and settled down on one elbow.

'Each one of you will visit the story of your life,' Aenais continued.

One more time, the high priestess looked at them intently, slowly turning her eyes from one GeeBee to the other. Her gaze seemed to go through and beyond them all.

'Everything will become clear soon enough. Just sit back and relax.'

And so, they all made themselves comfortable, each in their own way, and waited in anticipation for what was coming next.

'Close your eyes, and as you concentrate on my voice, begin to relax - relax - relaxing deeper and deeper.'

Aenais took some deep audible breaths, sighing gently as she breathed out.

'Allow your breath to flow in and flow out - naturally - without forcing anything.'

Her soft, slow, soothing, voice created a sense of safety, calmness and relaxation.

'Now breathe deeply enough so that you can really hear the sound of your breath. Notice what it feels like, as the air goes in through your nostrils and comes out over your lips.'

Aenais paused for a little longer this time.

'That's it - in and out - in and out.'

Everyone's eyelids started to feel heavy, so very heavy.

'Now, become aware of the vast, empty space all around you.'

Aenais continued her soothing monologue for quite some time, talking of space, time, sacred centres and all kinds of strange things. Until finally, the Gee Bees could no longer fight their weariness, and slowly began to drift away on a soft cloud of sleep.

'You will each now enter your very own Chamber of Wishes.'

Just as Aenais said, they each found themselves standing at the entrance to another chamber, with a sweet smell of jasmine permeating the air. Five separate chambers, one for each GeeBee. Smaller in size than the Golden Chamber this room had no columns. Neither did it have a seating area.

The far end of the chamber was lined with a huge crystal bookcase, running the full length of the wall. Hundreds and hundreds of books covering every inch of the wall space, from floor to ceiling.

'Welcome to our Chamber of Wishes,' came a different voice from next to each explorer.

As the GeeBees turned sideways they saw, instead of their friends, a face that was even more familiar. In their very own Chamber of Wishes, they each found themselves standing next to their very own Whisper; hovering just above the floor and flashing a beaming smile.

Jack had his identical Jack Whisper. Akira, her Akira Whisper. Holly, her Holly Whisper. Finn, his Finn Whisper. And mirroring Isabelle was her very own, beloved Whisper.

The GeeBees could all see and hear but could not speak. But they didn't have to. Since their Whisper was a part of them, all their thoughts and all their feelings could be transferred telepathically without the use of the spoken word.

Through the air came the sound of chimes, *tinkle - tinkle - ting-a-ling*. Despite the astonishing turn of events, it all seemed somehow just right that they should meet their Whisper. Right here, right now.

'Every one of these books has your name written on it, and

contains information about the story of your life,' said Whisper.

Every single detail of every single event that had gone before, had been recorded here. Every decision the children had ever made, every good or bad emotion they had felt, every word they had spoken, every thought that had ever crossed their mind was recorded in these books.

'The books also speak of your gifts, talents and unique qualities,' Whisper said lovingly.

A silvery-white light began to emanate from the crystal bookcase. Running its full length, were multiple shelves and three small drawers, set bang in the middle.

'Can you feel the one on the left calling you to open it?' asked Whisper.

The explorers could indeed hear a very soft, singing voice coming from the drawer on the left, calling out their name. They each felt an inexplicable urge to open it.

'Hidden in that drawer is the freedom from all that you lack and the abundance that you deserve,' said Whisper.

And so, they each opened the drawer on the left, reaching in and pulling out a faded cream-coloured envelope, with their name on it. They opened it they found a letter with the following hand-written message:

Do not spend your energy on negative thoughts, as that only takes you away from loving yourself. You have the freedom to choose thoughts that will help you blossom and become even greater than you are.

This is your birthright and yours to have at this very moment.

If this is your desire, then tear this paper up and in so doing, all the negative thoughts that limit you from being your authentic self will disappear.

Finally, say thank you three times and close the drawer.

The GeeBees each mulled over the most unusual message,

to ensure they had understood it properly. When they felt ready, they tore the paper into tiny pieces and threw them into the air like confetti.

'Thank you, thank you, thank you,' they each said, and closed the drawer.

The same weird tingling sensation went through all of them, flowing in through the top of their heads like a warm current, streaming right down into their feet.

'Now, the middle one,' said Whisper.

Each GeeBee opened the second drawer where there was another envelope, again with each of their names written on it. Here they found, not only a piece of paper, but a pendant on a chain. Circular in shape, the bronze pendant was embossed with the image of the Argead Star.

The message read as follows:

The journey of self-improvement is meant for those who are ready to accept 100% responsibility for the results in their lives. For you to move on, you need to have understood every Life Secret that you have received here on Aydagar and agree to incorporate your learnings into your everyday life.

This pendant will remind you of all you have learnt, so keep it safe with you always.

You are now ready to move onto to higher levels of self-awareness.

If this is what you desire, then fold this paper, return it to the drawer and put on your necklace.

Say thank you three times.

The GeeBees read this message over several times, to make sure they agreed with every single word.

'Go ahead, close the drawer when you're ready,' said Whisper.

So, they each folded the paper into four, slipped it into the envelope and placed it back into the drawer.

'Thank you, thank you, thank you,' they all uttered

once again.

The explorers each slipped the chain over their heads and held the pendant between their fingers. Apart from the image of the Argead Star, there were three simple letters engraved on the reverse side: GBE.

'And now, last but not least,' said Whisper, gesturing towards the remaining drawer.

Once again, there was an envelope with their individual names written on it. However, this piece of paper was blank; with no words or instructions written on it at all.

The GeeBees gave a puzzled look towards their Whispers.

'You have been found worthy of three wishes' said the five Whispers.

The paper that each explorer was holding was intentionally left blank, for this was where their three wishes would be recorded. They could wish for anything their hearts desired and it would be granted to them.

'Take your time and choose your wishes wisely,' said Whisper.

A zillion unconnected half-thoughts swarmed like busy bees through the minds of each GeeBee; thoughts about all the things they could be or do or have in their lives.

'When you're ready, state your three wishes clearly in your head and have faith that they will come true,' said Whisper.

It didn't take long for Isabelle, Akira, Holly, Jack and Finn to think up their wishes.

'Go ahead, listen to the voice inside your head,' Whisper said, encouragingly.

With no need to say a thing out loud, the words spilled out of their minds and fell directly onto the blank paper.

Isabelle's Whisper smiled lovingly as Isabelle's three wishes gradually became visible in golden ink.

'I wish to always say what I'm thinking, without being scared. I wish to always feel strong and courageous like I feel now. I just wish, to be happy'.

She needed nothing more, and she wanted nothing less.

As soon as they had all made their wishes, the GeeBees said their final, 'Thank you, thank you, thank you.'

Slipping the papers back into their envelopes, all five explorers ceremoniously placed them back into the drawer.

All of a sudden, a burst of bright light surrounded each GeeBee and their Whisper, sending a ring of intense light radiating outwards in an ever-widening circle. Instantly, they felt their legs being lifted from the ground by an invisible force. Suspended in the air, just a few inches off the ground, they each hovered at the same level as their Whisper.

After what seemed like ages, the blinding light began to flicker, gradually growing dimmer and dimmer. All five Whispers started moving closer to their GeeBees until finally they merged to become one whole; part of each other once again. The light gradually dimmed until it entirely ceased.

After a long silence, Aenais's soft voice could be heard counting backwards.

'Ten, nine, eight ... three, two, one.'

The high priestess rang a small, brass bell - *da-ding, da-ding, da-ding*.

'And when you're ready, you can return to the room and open your eyes.'

As Isabelle slowly opened her heavy eyelids, she wondered if it had all been just a lovely dream.

'Did you see your Whisper?' she whispered to Holly.

'Yes, I did,' said Holly, slowly sitting herself up on the couch.

'I thought it was my imagination, but it was so real,'

Finn said.

'Me too, and mine spoke to me,' Akira said.

'So, did mine,' said Holly.

Still somewhere between a state of dreaming and consciousness, Jack continued to keep his eyes closed but was nevertheless following the conversation.

'Mine went back inside me,' he said.

'Same here,' said Akira, examining her body.

And so, the Great Budding Explorers talked and talked, non-stop, about what had happened just before.

'It's incredible, we all went through the same thing,' said Holly.

'That means, it must've really happened,' said Isabelle.

14

PARTING OF THE WAYS

Maybe it had been a dream, maybe it hadn't.

'Do dreams leave a smell behind them,' asked Holly.

She sniffed the air around her and could detect the fragrance of sweet flowers. She grabbed a tuft of her hair between her fingers, lifted it to her nose and took a whiff.

'Do dreams leave you with this,' said Isabelle, holding her Argead Star pendant in front of her.

The gasps of astonishment blended into the silence, as the GeeBees thought back to their experience.

'Anoixe tora,' said Aenais, commanding the door to open.

The grand door to the Golden Chamber creaked open and Aenais walked out, followed by the five Great Budding Explorers. By now, the night had given away to the first light of dawn. The stars were fading and even the moon had changed colour to a soft pinkish-white.

The explorers ran out to meet the Captain who was waiting for them under the gazibo. Still very much bewildered by the events that had unfolded, they sat down next to him and excitedly related the events of the night.

'There was a sunken sofa,' said Holly

'And a floating chimney,' Finn butted in excitedly.

'And we all met our Whispers,' said Akira.

Captain M listened to their ramblings about a hundred different things; the Chamber of Wishes, the library and the fact that they had all shared the same experience but in a different dimension. Until at last, he had no choice but to stop the full flow of discourse.

'The stars are exactly as they should be,' he told the GeeBees, looking up into the sky.

After what seemed like an eternity since their exploration had begun, the time had come for them to journey back home.

'So, what exactly will our mode of transport be?' Akira asked the Captain.

'Probably the way we came, by sea,' said Finn.

'Oh yes,' said Jack. 'I forgot all about the Discovery.'

Captain M simply shook his head in a negative response. Standing up, he smoothed down his clothes and made his way to the centre of the open courtyard. He then stood quite still, scanning the clear night sky.

The explorers walked up behind him and gaped as they saw two black blotches appearing on the horizon.

'What's that?' asked Isabelle.

'The nemesis of love,' whispered the Captain.

'That doesn't sound very promising,' said Akira.

 The dark shapes spread, growing larger and larger until the GeeBees saw not shadows but flying creatures.

'Is that what I think it is?' said Holly.

'It's - the Mind Monsters,' said Jack.

'I thought we got rid of them,' said Finn.

'They're coming straight for us,' said Akira, taking a few steps backwards.

'We should take cover,' said Holly.

They all watched intently for a few seconds, as the Mind Monsters flew swiftly and strongly towards them.

'What should we do?' said Akira.

'Run for it, probably,' Jack said.

'Or maybe we should stand our ground,' said Isabelle.

The Captain splayed his arms sideways and turned his head slightly towards the GeeBees.

'Do not move from what you know is right,' he said in a loud whisper.

'This is no time for brain teasers, Captain M,' said Akira.

It was clear to her that if they didn't react quickly, the monsters would soon be upon them.

'Stay close and face them head on,' the Captain repeated in plainer terms.

Everyone shuffled a little nearer their guide, until they were all standing just inches apart from one other.

In almost no time at all, Apotihia, the Monster of Failure, came within a few feet of the Gee Bees; towering over them with her emerald-green, flapping wings. She landed with astonishing grace, gnashing her spider fangs at Jack. Hot, green mucus trickled from her nostrils and she let out a menacing, ear-piercing screech of protest, that echoed around the courtyard.

Agnosto, the Monster of the Unknown, came in just behind. Landing heavily with a thunderous thump on his strong powerful legs, he made the earth around them tremble. For a short while, he flared his blood-red wings into two giant crescents and arched his tail up behind. When he finally folded his wings, he stretched his long neck out towards Isabelle, snorting loudly.

'I'm not scared of you,' said Isabelle.

She neither flinched nor winced, but instead stared determinedly at the creature, as he swayed uneasily from side to side.

'Kato tora,' said the Captain, commanding the monsters to sit down.

His words were like a magic spell. Both creatures dropped heavily to the ground, turning slightly onto their heaving sides. Apart from a series of loud grunts, they sat as still as obedient dogs, quietening down. Their heavy breathing became shallower and shallower until it was almost inaudible.

'I didn't expect that to go quite so well,' said Jack with a glint of humour in his eye.

He looked at Apotihia warily, wondering if he was going to be somehow sprayed with green slime.

'I think they know who's in charge,' said Isabelle, raising her chin slightly.

'This is all fine and good,' said Akira. 'But what's this got to do with our return?'

'Why not use the very forces that you once feared, but have now conquered?' said the Captain.

'You mean, them?' asked Akira.

It was only a matter of seconds before they all realised that the Mind Monsters could be their first-class ticket back home.

'Awesome,' said Finn.

'But how?' queried Jack.

'They're so wild,' Holly groaned.

'But they're not as wild as we thought they were,' said Isabelle.

'You've seen that your mind can be both your best friend

and your worst enemy,' the Captain reminded them.

'Yeah, I learnt that first-hand,' said Jack.

'Imagine flying home on your friendly Mind Monsters,' said the Captain.

'Whaaat?' said Holly.

'I've ridden a horse before,' said Finn, 'but riding a Mind Monster would be incredible.'

'As Izzy said before, you're the ones in charge now,' the Captain said.

'It can't be very different from riding a horse,' Isabelle commented.

'Precisely. If you're not holding the reins tightly, the monster will pull you in the direction it wants with no regard for what you want,' said the Captain.

'But if we pull on the reins whenever we want, then we can keep the monster under control,' said Isabelle, following the Captain's gist.

As she spoke, she felt Agnosto's gaze on her. He looked more like a sleepy cat, than the threatening monster she came face to face with in the Monster Caves. The monster lifted his huge head and quite unexpectedly spoke in a very husky voice.

'I can help you.'

'What's the right way to respond to a Mind Monster?' Isabelle asked herself.

'Go on, ask him if he can help us?' Holly whispered.

'Can you really help us?' Isabelle asked.

'Yes,' said the monster, the corners of his eyes crinkling in a welcoming smile. 'I am very much at your service, my lady.'

He lowered his head in reverence to the person that had so courageously stood up to him. Following suit, Apotihia also bowed her head towards Jack.

Isabelle felt a rush of excitement. Reaching her hand out tentatively towards Agnosto's forehead, she touched him ever so lightly with her fingertips. When she sensed that everything was okay, Isabelle began stroking the leathery skin of his long snout.

Agnosto's eyes turned an amber yellow colour and narrowed slightly in response. Then he began to make a deep purring sound.

'He sounds like a cat,' said Jack.

'He's lovely,' said Isabelle. 'Not at all scary.'

Isabelle turned around to look at her friends, with a truly contented expression on her face; her fear and insecurity, no longer able to rob her of her confidence.

'Once again Isabelle, you have shown yourself that it is within your power to tame your Mind Monsters,' said the Captain.

'What can I ask him for?' Isabelle asked him.

'Ask of them whatever you want.'

'We can always fly down to the Power Coast,' said Finn.

'Or even, all the way back home,' said Jack.

'Can we really do that?' Isabelle asked.

The Captain nodded and smiled.

Isabelle stared at Agnosto. He had an odd look in his eyes, as if there was an inexplicable connection between them.

'Can you please take us home?' she said in a low, but unfaltering voice.

Agnosto's pupils started dilating into bands of orange and black.

'As you wish,' he answered.

'Yes - monster riding,' Jack said.

'Let's get going then,' said Finn.

The time had finally come for the GeeBees to journey back home. Isabelle's heart tugged at the thought of leaving Captain M and she stared at him, not saying a word. The Captain smiled from ear to ear and opened his arms wide, pulling them all into a group hug.

Isabelle choked but managed to blurt out, 'We are coming back, aren't we?'

Before letting go of them, the Captain reminded them of the oath they had taken in the Chamber of Wishes; to make their learnings on Aydagar part of their lives.

'The paper that we put back into the second drawer,' said Akira.

'That's right,' said the Captain. 'Walk your talk and you'll be back in no time.'

'Gotcha boss' Jack said and winked.

'Then we'll discover more Life Secrets, right?' said Isabelle.

'There's always more to learn Izzy,' said the Captain. 'Always plenty more.'

Isabelle quickly bounced out of her sadness, knowing that she could and would be back. And without further ado, she slowly began to climb up Agnosto's tail and onto his back.

'Go as far forward as you can,' said the Captain.

Crouching low to keep her balance, Isabelle inched forward and sat down close to the nape of his neck.

'Let's ride together,' she called out to Finn.

He immediately scrambled onto Agnosto's back, moving up closer towards Isabelle.

'He's quite soft for a dragon,' said Isabelle, stroking him.

'I've never stroked a dragon before, so I wouldn't know,' said Finn.

They both giggled as they made themselves comfortable

for the flight.

Jack turned to Akira and Holly and said,

'Follow me to business class.'

The three of them walked up to Apotihia's head, and wedged themselves between the creature's neck and shoulder blades, their legs dangling either side.

No sooner were they all seated, than the scales around the necks of both monsters started to grow out lengthways, enveloping the lower part of the GeeBee's bodies. Their legs were now clamped tightly against the creatures' backs, fixed to the spot and ready for the flight ahead.

'Did you see that?' asked Holly.

'They're like shackles,' said Jack, tugging and pulling at his legs.

'Our very own monster seat belt,' quipped Akira, stroking the polished scales covering her legs.

The Great Budding Explorers were now ready for take-off and they hung on tight as the monsters jerked their bodies forward and stood up.

'Farewell, my friends,' said the Captain.

He stepped towards each one of them, holding them by the hand and doing his familiar circular motion over their open palms.

'Thanks for a fantastic time, Captain M,' called out Finn.

'Yes, it was really great,' said Akira.

'Thank you for everything,' said Holly, smiling and waving.

'Bye Captain M,' said Jack, giving a salute.

The Captain took it in turns to bid goodbye to everyone and then walked up to Isabelle. He held her hand tightly and looked deep into her eyes.

'Izzy, you made this exploration effiktable for everyone. It was a great honour to meet you.'

'Nice to meet you too, Captain M,' said Isabelle.

Her eyes welled with happy tears as the Captain took a few steps backwards.

'Fair winds,' he called out loudly.

The Mind Monsters reared onto their hind legs, unfurled their wings and began to flap them slowly. As the air flowed around their wings, they began to pick up speed, kicking up a cloud of dust like a bull in a rodeo.

In the final moments before they took to the air the Captain called up to them,

'Listen out for your Whisper and remember, anything is effiktable if you really want it.'

He gave them a wistful wave and made a very long bow.

As the Mind Monsters rose into the air, Isabelle looked down and gave one last wave to the Captain. She mouthed another 'bye-bye' and continued to look down at him, as they rose higher and higher into the sky, until he was no longer in sight.

Aydagar gradually fell away behind them. The fields stretched far and wide, whilst the jungle crept over large parts of the island like a never-ending carpet. Even Arkadia Falls was visible from up here.

Isabelle wondered if she would get to see the Aiads and Aryads next time round.

'I know I will,' she muttered to herself. 'Anything is effiktable.'

For a short while the monsters flew in circles well-above Avaton Temple.

'It looks like a playground,' squealed Holly excitedly.

'Look, there's the Monster Caves,' called out Jack.

'They look so small from up here,' said Holly.

'There's the Discovery,' shouted Finn, pointing to the bay off the Power Coast.

'Oh, yes,' said Akira. 'It's incredible up here.'

Heading south by south east, Aydagar soon disappeared completely as they drifted into a thick blanket of fluffy, white clouds. Only a few minutes into their flight, Agnosto told them all to hold on tight. The monsters pointed their heads upwards and started a steep vertical climb towards the dome of the sky.

The GeeBees leant forward and wrapped their arms around the creatures' necks, gripping onto the scales as tightly as they could. For a long moment it seemed as if they were suspended in air and couldn't get any higher. When suddenly, the dragons rolled over backwards, doing an impressive acrobatic loop-the-loop.

A chorus of excited squeals, '*awwws*' and '*aaahs*' filled the air until they returned to a horizontal position.

'We're better than the Red Arrows,' said Finn at the top of his voice.

'I thought we were going to fall off,' squealed Holly.

'*Yee-haa*,' Jack yowled. 'Do it again.'

'No, no, don't,' said Akira.

She swallowed hard, trying to keep the contents of her stomach in place.

Everything was seemingly unreal up here but given the past few days, nothing seemed out of the realm of possibility. Somewhere in between the sky and the earth the explorers became lost in a vast emptiness of white space. Their eyes began to droop, until they were soon carried into a dreamy oblivion.

Isabelle's head fell drowsily onto the nape of Agnosto's neck and she yawned sleepily, longing for the warmth of her fluffy duvet. But the strange sensation of her head resting against something cold pulled her out of her dream state.

Scarcely more than half awake, she realised that she was sitting with her knees drawn tightly up against her chest, and her head was resting against the window frame. She sat up with a jolt when she heard a voice saying,

'Wake up.'

Slowly she peeked through her still heavy eyelids to see a blur of a smile.

'Whisper?' she said, forcing herself to blink.

'No silly, it's me,' said Holly, giggling.

Isabelle's heart pounded and forced her body into motion. Sitting up straight, she realised she was sitting on the windowsill, in the same place where it all begun.

'Was it a dream?' she asked. 'Was I asleep?'

'Not unless I was too,' answered Holly.

She put her hand inside the top of her t-shirt and pulled out a necklace with a coin-like round pendant hanging from it. It glowed with light as she dangled it in front of her face.

'It's the Argead Star,' said Isabelle, catching her breath a little.

Lightning Source UK Ltd.
Milton Keynes UK
UKHW010627100621
385271UK00001B/288